Life.

Maryellen Winkler

MW00643691

CRUISING
TO
DEATH

An
Emily Menotti
Mystery

by

MARYELLEN WINKLER

Also by Maryellen Winkler:

The Disappearance of Darcie Malone

What Killed Rosie?

Cruising to Death
Copyright 2016, Maryellen Winkler
All rights reserved.

ISBN
978-1-935751-39-7 (paperback)
978-1-935751-40-3 (eBook)

Published by
Scribbulations LLC
Kennett Square, Pennsylvania
U.S.A.

This is a work of fiction. Names, characters, places, and incidents either are the product of the author's imagination or are used fictitiously, and any resemblance to any actual persons, living or dead, events, or locales is entirely coincidental.

This story is dedicated to the members of my book club whose original welcome and continuing support have been a blessing to me for over thirty-five years.

Acknowledgments

I would like to thank my friend, Donna Moe,
who once again agreed to be my First Look Editor
and Grace Spampinato, who offered
invaluable support and advice.

The world is full of beautiful ladies

Singing sad songs,

Luring not sailors but themselves

Into lives of quiet despair.

-mew

CRUISE DAY ONE

SUNDAY

CHAPTER ONE

The Woman in the Window

I stood on the pier attached to the terminal and viewed the cruise ship docked in front of me. It was larger than I had imagined. The massive steel hull, rising up out of the dank Hudson River, displayed three rows of blank portholes. Above the lower deck rose multiple levels of empty balconies. On the upper decks, glass walls reflected the gray sky.

The ship's length was a thousand feet, the size of three football fields. I counted fifteen stories visible from where I stood. There were no passengers on board yet, and in the foggy morning, it appeared deserted.

In the damp early hours, there was nothing festive about the ship—no strings of party lights nor illuminated palm trees gracing the upper decks. The famed *Galleon of the Galaxy* looked more like a medieval fortress. If I stared hard enough, I could almost see a young woman held prisoner behind one of the bottom rows of portholes. Her hair was pale blond, with her face similarly fair and devoid of color. She raised her hand in a wave to get my attention. Inside my head I heard her words, "Help me!"

I was in no mood to be led on another ghostly, wild-goose chase like the one I had recently been on, summoned by the apparition of an old friend. Today, I was embarking on my first cruise with a group of women from a local book club. I was looking forward to poolside margaritas, long afternoon naps, and cocktail hours with elegant martinis followed by five-star dinners. How dare this unknown spirit beckon to me!

As I argued with her in my mind, she faded from view. I shook my head in disbelief. I was imagining things. The vision was just the result of too much early morning coffee and not enough toast. I dismissed her and went to look for my friend, Melinda.

CHAPTER TWO

The Wayward Sisters

They called themselves the Wayward Sisters which sounds wicked fun, but they were actually quite ordinary women who had formed a book club in Wayward, New Hampshire, a few miles down the road from my home in Swansea.

One of their members had gotten married the day before, and she and her new husband were part of the book club's annual cruise to the Eastern Caribbean. I thought it odd to share your honeymoon with your book club, but I learned the cruise and the honeymoon had originally been planned as two separate events.

The member, Phoebe, was getting married, but she and her new husband could not afford an expensive honeymoon. "Duncan is paying tons of alimony," Phoebe explained.

Meanwhile, the Wayward Sisters had planned their cruise, reserving four cabins at double occupancy. At the last minute, one couple and one single woman had begged off, leaving three empty spots. These were offered to Phoebe; her then fiancé, Duncan Blumen; and me, with tickets and transportation already arranged. We all accepted, grateful the group rate made this vacation adventure affordable.

"We have to wait inside," Melinda's voice interrupted my thoughts. "Everyone is here, and we've got seats together while we wait to board."

Melinda was the book club member who had suggested including me. Earlier in the year, I'd broken up with a cherished man, and I was still grieving his loss. She hoped the cruise would cheer me up.

I followed her back into the cavernous building where rows of plastic molded seats held approximately two thousand passengers now separated from their luggage and waiting for permission to board.

Melinda pointed to our tickets and explained that passengers were sorted by color. Yellow ticket holders sat in one section together, as did green, blue, pink, purple, and red. Your ticket color determined your stateroom choice and rank in the pecking order. The eight of us held green tickets, signifying double occupancy staterooms with small balconies.

The newlyweds, Phoebe and Duncan, sat huddled together, clasping hands. Phoebe's blonde head was leaning against Duncan's tonsure of graying brown fringe as they smiled blissfully into space. Phoebe had been divorced for many years and was a recently retired preschool teacher. Duncan still worked as a financial officer at the local hospital.

Melinda beckoned me to a seat between her and Sylvia. As she moved her knees sideways to allow us to enter the row, Sylvia frowned at the honeymoon couple seated in front of her. Sylvia Marsh was a wilted soul of fifty plus years who worked with me, although in a different department, at Metrobank NH, Inc. She'd lost her husband to cancer three years earlier, and she still wore her grief like a lingering scent of perfume: "eau de douleur."

Next to Sylvia sat Jane and Rick Smith, the odd couple. Jane loved people, animals, and plants—any living thing that needed nurturing. She had a heart as big as her zaftig hips and chest. She owned an arts and crafts shop in downtown Swansea, and the locals flocked to her classes every holiday season to fashion wreaths, baskets, center pieces, and other handmade gifts.

Rick was the athletic instructor and coach at Swansea Regional High School. He was golden haired and faintly muscular, with a pencil-thin mustache and hard blue eyes. Although I didn't know this couple well, I'd heard stories of Rick's OCD neatness and his garage-turned-gym that was cleaner than any garage or gym had a right to be.

Jane suffered from asthma, which was her excuse for why she couldn't exercise and lose weight. She pooh-poohed all advice and doctor's warnings. She was "who she was," she would tell you, and "completely content with that." You had to envy her attitude, if not her body. Someone had once casually mentioned that Rick had dated the slender Phoebe back in high school. Rumor also had it that he and Jane were unable to have children and that Rick took this as a personal defeat. I imagined what conversations might be like between the overly health-conscious Rick and his devil-may-care wife and wondered if he ever regretted choosing Jane.

Last in our party was Liz Spode, a career nurse, who also worked at our local hospital and had never married. She sat quietly among us and did crossword puzzles as we waited for our section to be called to board. Her brown hair was streaked with silver, a graceful counterpoint to her youthfully smooth skin. She had a slight, athletic frame that was the envy of most women I knew.

I'd heard she dated now and then, but never anyone for long. She had two cats to keep her company on winter evenings and was the book club's most voracious reader.

"Green." The voice over the loudspeaker burst through my thoughts.

We all stood up and allowed ourselves to be herded out the door and onto the wide, high-fenced gangplank, clutching our newly issued photo IDs. Handing mine over to the Security personnel waiting for us on the main deck of the ship, I watched them scan the IDs into a small machine and carefully put mine safely away when it was returned. Melinda had told me that, once in the Caribbean, they would be scanned each time we disembarked and once more on our return to the ship. This way Security always knew who had returned to the ship and who had not.

Next we were directed inside to a crowded lobby. Multiple crystal chandeliers, reflecting on the marble walls and floor, provided light like that of a thousand suns. I stood still to let my eyes adjust to the brightness. The noise of the throng already inside was deafening.

"Keep going," someone admonished us, and I asked Melinda, "What now?"

"We take the elevators up to our staterooms. Ours are on deck eight. Follow me."

"Will our luggage be waiting for us?"

Melinda laughed.

"I'm afraid not. We'll be lucky if they deliver it by dinnertime."

We pushed through the crowd into a hallway with banks of elevators on both sides, four on the right and four on the left. There didn't seem to be an order to the boarding. I saw Liz and Sylvia vanish into an open car and wondered how they'd managed to get so far ahead of us.

We waited amid the crush of passengers as elevator cars ascended and then descended back to us on deck four. The waiting crowd diminished with agonizing slowness. Finally, an elevator door opened in front of us like the jaws of a huge fish. Melinda and I rushed inside to secure a spot, along with Phoebe, Duncan, and six strangers.

"I guess you newlyweds don't mind being smashed together, but it's a little awkward for the rest of us," Melinda smiled.

"Well, it's not too bad," Duncan replied, "but I'd prefer to be alone if Phoebe and I are going to be bosom buddies."

"I'll take you anyway I can get you," Phoebe teased, with a wink to Melinda and me.

Our eyes tracked the changing numbers above the door as we traveled up from deck four to deck eight, stopping along the way to disgorge occupants at each floor. At eight, we four were the only ones left. We found ourselves in a small alcove with narrow corridors branching out in front of us and to the left and right. Melinda and I were in stateroom 8328. Duncan and Phoebe were in 8330, right next door. The small directional signs told us 8000 to 8099 were straight ahead, 8100 to 8299 were to our left, and 8300 to 8499 were to our right. We turned right.

It was a bit of a hike but we eventually found our staterooms, glad we weren't required to make any turns or drag luggage along. Opening the door with my photo ID card, I was pleasantly surprised at the space that Melinda and I would be sharing.

Immediately on either side of the door were a closet and a bathroom. I poked my head into the bathroom. It was a study in the efficient use of space with a shower that looked barely big enough to handle a small woman of moderate weight. I smiled to myself as I imagined portly passengers — or more specifically Jane — washing one half of themselves at a time. Luckily Jane was a person with lots of good humor.

The rest of the stateroom was roughly the size of my old college dorm room, and I expected Melinda and I would be fine. Two single beds, two dressers, one desk, and a small sofa made up the furnishings. The outside wall was a sliding glass door that opened onto a small, covered balcony with two white plastic chairs and a table. A high railing ensured our protection from falling.

Inside, a flower arrangement of white and yellow lilies sat on our tiny coffee table with a blue ribbon and note that read: "Welcome aboard!" This completed the cozy picture.

Phoebe and Duncan had first peeked at our room, then quickly went to theirs. Melinda and I soon followed them, and I noted that their room was exactly like ours except decorated in shades of mauve where ours was blue.

"Oh no!" Phoebe groaned. "Twin beds!"

"I'm sure you'll figure something out," Melinda grinned.

I commented on the sameness of the rooms, even down to the flower arrangement. However, underneath their vase was an envelope addressed to "The Newlyweds." Duncan opened it and read the message as we all watched his expression change from smile to frown. When he was done, he handed it to Phoebe. Phoebe read out loud:

Fair of skin is not pure of heart
Blue eyes see little in the dark
When blood turns black and eyes burn green
Beware the secrets now unseen.

CHAPTER THREE
A Tour of the Ship

"I don't like this," Duncan said.

"We both have blue eyes," Phoebe pointed out. "Whoever wrote this seems to think we're blind to something. Are you hiding anything, dear?"

"Only the wives overseas," he deadpanned.

"I expect to be treated like the First Lady of your heart," Phoebe responded with a kiss to his cheek.

"Who would write such a thing?" I said, in an effort to refocus on the nasty note.

"Perhaps it wasn't meant for us," Duncan suggested. "Perhaps it's been left after the last occupants."

"I don't think so," Melinda frowned.

"Do you think someone from our book club wrote this?" Phoebe asked.

"No, this note is almost a threat," Melinda said. She took the note from Phoebe and touched it carefully with her fingertips, as if contact would yield more information.

"We'll ask the others at lunch," Phoebe suggested. "Now can my new husband and I have a few moments alone?"

"Of course," Melinda said, placing the note back on the small table with the flowers. "Emily and I will explore the ship. We'll meet in the dining room at one thirty."

After making a quick stop in our stateroom, Melinda and I hurried off to discover where the pool and dining rooms were. We rode the elevator to deck twelve and found the pool nestled in between the casual dining room at one end and the gym, spa, and salon at the other. The pool was Olympic size with a slide at one end and a Tahitian bar at the opposite end. Two hot tub pools were labeled "For Adults Only" and were already filled with giggling preteen girls. Melinda pointed out the promenade, a teak boardwalk that encompassed the deck.

Back on the elevator, we exited on deck eleven, where we found ourselves at the top of an atrium that extended down through decks ten and nine. Standing at the railing, we were eye level with three crystal chandeliers that lit the area below.

On deck eleven, specialty restaurants featuring Italian, Asian, and steak house cuisine were dotted around the edges of the atrium. Toward the front of the ship we found a movie theater, and situated at the back, was the formal dining room where dinner would be served every evening if one chose to forgo the restaurants. Tucked in one corner was a small library, populated with magazines, paperback books, and plump armchairs, but empty of people.

We descended one level via a wide staircase, shining with steps of white marble veined in gold. The staircase swept in s-curves from deck eleven down to ten and again from ten down to nine into an area Melinda called the Grand Gallery. Looking down we saw palm trees and tall ferns shading gurgling fountains. Only the stairway's Plexiglas side walls kept one from tumbling into the greenery below.

Taking in the sparkling chandeliers, gleaming marble, and melodious fountains, I felt transported to an exotic land. Diaphanous queens and stalwart princes could glide by at any moment. A fairy-tale romance might be even now flowering among the fronds.

On deck ten, we inspected dainty shops for clothing, toiletries, gifts, and duty-free liquor, all shut behind metal gates. A sign announced that the shops would remain closed while the ship was in port.

Taking up the entire front of the ship was a spacious casino, also closed. The silent machines, standing at attention with no lights blinking or bells ringing, looked like sleeping robot soldiers awaiting their call to battle. Reversing our steps and peeking down the corridors toward the aft, we guessed the larger and more expensive staterooms were located in the carpeted tunnels of the back deck.

Descending the staircase again to level nine, we found offices and two auditoriums, along with a coffee shop and empty lounges. Then it was back to the elevators where we learned that decks eight through five were entirely staterooms.

Deck four, the main deck, held more offices, shuttered shops, and another teak promenade—the one on which we had boarded the ship. The elevators didn't offer a stop at decks three or one. Melinda guessed these were crew-only decks that probably had their own elevators in a restricted area. Deck two was the infirmary.

Examining the floor plan next to the elevator to see if we had missed anything, we discovered an elevator in the front half of the ship that took us up to deck thirteen, which turned out to be a partial deck located above the prow.

When we arrived there, Melinda declared, "Party deck!" Every room was a bar, each having a different theme—Disco Nights, All That Jazz, Art Deco, and Old English Pub. Open already, the bars were filled with excited passengers, glasses in hand getting themselves into a holiday mood.

"No one's going thirsty on this cruise," I remarked.

"Wait until you see your liquor tab at the end of our vacation," Melinda joked. "It'll be twice the cost of your stateroom."

It was one thirty by this time, and we headed back to deck twelve to the casual dining restaurant where we said we'd meet the others. As we waded through the crowd in front of the entrance, I noticed service personnel stopping people as they entered and insisting they receive a squirt of hand sanitizer.

"Norovirus," I overheard one gentleman mutter. "Can't be too careful."

I held out my hands gladly.

Once sanitized, Melinda and I left the queue for the cafeteria style lunch and searched among the crowded tables for our friends. We found them at the very back where wraparound windows provided a view of the harbor. At the moment we arrived, everyone was admiring the two-carat, princess cut diamond on Phoebe's left hand. All, that is, except for Liz, who was ignoring them and picking at a small salad.

The diamond caught a ray of sun and sparkled with rainbow splendor. I drew in my own breath in admiration.

"How lovely," I remarked, at which Phoebe only smiled.

"You didn't wait for us!" Melinda wailed.

"Did you see that line?" Sylvia replied. "We weren't taking any chances that they might run out of food."

Jane snorted. "On a cruise? You've never seen so much food in your life. Just wait until the midnight buffet."

"Well...Emily and I are getting back in line. Keep our seats, okay?"

We returned to the now dwindling line. I was amazed at the selection of food: ham steaks, Asian vegetables and noodles, ziti with tomato sauce, hamburgers and cheeseburgers, three kinds of fish, and an array of lunch meats. Rolls, pita bread, taco shells, and white or whole wheat bread provided the daily requirement of carbohydrates.

In between the buffet and the tables were stations with salad, condiments, extra silverware, mugs, glasses, and beverages. I scooped up some mayo for my ham and cheese sandwich, grabbed a glass of lemonade, and headed back, disappointed there were no potato chips.

By the time I'd found my way to our table, Liz had finished her salad and was rising to leave.

"I'm going to change and hit the workout room," she announced. "Maybe I'll meet up with you guys later."

"Liz is trying to make this a healthy cruise," Sylvia observed. "Not a self-indulgent one like the rest of us."

"We brought all our pills, though," Phoebe observed, eyeing the scattered plastic boxes everyone seemed to have in front of them with squares marked SMTWRFS. If passengers couldn't tell we were all aged fifty plus from our faces, those little boxes were a dead giveaway. I saw a clear plastic bag of amber bottles poking out of Phoebe's bag.

"We figure we can eat and drink all we want if we keep up with our meds," Duncan laughed. "Phoebe doesn't take many, but I take a rainbow collection of these little things."

"And we couldn't leave them in our luggage or else we wouldn't get them until after dinner, so I've got to lug them around with me all day," Phoebe moaned. "I think men should start carrying purses."

Melinda, Liz, and I seemed to be the only ones without little plastic boxes—a testament to our healthy lifestyle, lucky parental genes, or sheer laziness.

"Well...Okay...See you all later," Liz said and got up to leave.

When she was out of sight, Sylvia said, "Liz told me she lost five pounds last month just to prepare for this cruise. She was very concerned there wasn't going to be any healthy foods she could enjoy."

"But she's already thin as a rail!" Phoebe exclaimed. "What does she weigh? Maybe a hundred pounds?"

"You know Liz," Jane spoke up, pulling a topaz shawl around her shoulders to ward off a sudden burst of air conditioning. "It's not so much the weight as exercising her willpower. She needs to be in control. Poor thing. I'm not sure what she gets out of that."

"Too bad she can't bottle that willpower and sell it," Rick said while digging into a tuna steak. "She'd make a fortune. I'd buy some and give it to Jane as a present. Hey, what's everybody doing this afternoon?"

With a sideways glance at her spouse, we could see that Jane had picked up on his criticism of her. An awkward silence followed as she chose not to respond.

Melinda finally volunteered that she was hoping to laze by the pool with a good book.

I seconded that idea.

"Me three, but I'm going to check in with Liz first and see if she wants to explore the ship," Sylvia said, taking a sip of black coffee.

"No need to ask the newlyweds," Jane said, gesturing toward Phoebe and Duncan. "I imagine they'll be taking long naps," she added with a quick wink at the two of them.

Before separating, we planned to meet at five o'clock for cocktails in the Art Deco bar on deck thirteen.

"I'll tell Liz," Sylvia said and left, along with Phoebe and Duncan.

"The newlyweds told us about that note with their flowers," Rick said when the honeymoon couple was out of earshot. "Who do you think wrote it?"

"I've no idea," Melinda said. "But I'm worried. It's not a pleasant omen for the start of a honeymoon cruise."

"Well...I think we'll catch up with the others," Rick looked at Jane, and they rose from the table.

Melinda and I stayed behind to finish our lunch.

Relaxing after eating, Melinda said, "Let's go back to the atrium for a sec. It's so beautiful. I want another glimpse of it, and I thought I saw a place where I can grab a cup of tea and a cookie later."

Not wanting to wait for the elevator, we decided to take the stairs down to bottom of the atrium. After a few minutes, we found a café that was closed, like the rest of the shops and the casino. We spotted a large menu mounted on the back wall featuring the café's various coffees, exotic teas, and a selection of cookies and scones.

"At least I know where to head when my blood sugar is dropping," Melinda grinned.

We were on our way back to the elevators when we heard loud voices at the top steps of the Grand Staircase on deck ten. We looked up to see the rest of our party and a crowd of others starting down the steps. Suddenly, there was a commotion as Phoebe seemed to lose her footing and grab for the railing. She couldn't quite reach it. Then I saw arms flail—I couldn't tell whose—and a shouted "Oh! Oh!" The next thing I knew, Phoebe was tumbling down the steps, arms and legs at odd angles. The passengers below her seemed to sense the danger just in time to steady themselves and avoid falling into her as she bumped past them. I held my breath in horror, fearing the worst.

Phoebe came to rest on her rear end at the bottom of the staircase, her back against the lower leg of a man in a gray sweater and black pants.

"I thought I was in heaven just being on this ship," the man said to her as he helped her up. "And now an angel has fallen at my feet. Are you okay?"

"Yes, I think so. Thank you," Phoebe replied, brushing off her ivory sweater and pale linen slacks.

"My name is Elvis..." he continued, including a surname that sounded like a string of consonants ending with an *i*.

Nosy passengers elbowed their way closer to Phoebe, crowding out Elvis and asking Phoebe if she had broken any bones. Duncan, Rick, Jane, Sylvia, and Liz hurried down the remaining steps and pushed their way through the crowd to where Phoebe was now laughing nervously. She shook her fair head and rubbed her arms and shoulders.

"I'm okay, really, I'm okay," she told the group. "It was these stupid tall sandals." She held out a delicate white foot in braided, platform soles. "Someone jostled me, my foot twisted, and then it fell right off the side of the shoe. I guess they're not the right footwear for walking up and down steps."

"How's your head?" Duncan asked, gazing at her with grave concern. "You might have a concussion."

"Yes, you should get it checked out at the infirmary," Melinda added. "Liz, you're a nurse. What do you think?"

Liz felt around Phoebe's head in a professional manner.

"Did you bump it in your fall?" she asked. "I don't feel any raised spots."

"No, I don't think so," Phoebe said. "It was mostly my elbows and derrière that took the beating...and my pride. I'm sure I'll be fine. Let's go, Duncan! I'm ready for a nap."

"You shouldn't go to sleep right after bumping your head," Liz told her.

"I'm not planning on sleeping," she smiled.

"Gotcha," Liz replied.

Without another word, Duncan and Phoebe left us, strolling off hand in hand.

"Have fun!" I called to their retreating forms.

"I've changed my mind," Liz said, also changing the subject. "I'm going to the gym to see if there's a free machine now. They were all taken earlier. See you later." She walked in the opposite direction.

"You know, I'm ready for a nap myself," Jane said.

"I'll join you," Rick said.

Without waiting to see what the rest of us planned to do, they sauntered off together.

"I'm with you guys," Sylvia said to Melinda and me.

We all decided to return to our rooms.

On deck eight, Sylvia turned to the opposite side of ship to her stateroom as we headed the other way toward ours. When she was out of earshot, I said to Melinda, "Phoebe thinks she was accidentally jostled but maybe she was pushed. Remember that note?"

"Hard to tell," Melinda replied. "It was pretty crowded there at the top. Let's keep our eyes open."

Just as we arrived at our cabin, a voice came over the loudspeaker:

"Welcome aboard the *Galleon of the Galaxy*. This is your captain speaking, Nielsen Bonaparte (he pronounced it Bon-a-par-tey). We will have a muster station drill at four o'clock sharp. Please read the instructions in your stateroom. Everyone is required to attend unless you are handicapped, in which case you will proceed to the casual dining room on deck twelve. We will read the passenger list, and if you are not present, someone will come to your stateroom to escort you to your muster station.

"You are required to wear your life jackets to the drill. They're located under your bed or in your closet. Please familiarize yourselves with how they fit and how they are deployed.

"After our drill, the ship will leave port promptly at five o'clock. We cannot wait for any passengers who have failed to arrive. Please keep this in mind for all future departures. Thank you."

"Wow, he's tough!" I said, surprised.

"Members of the Coast Guard will be on board to observe the drill," Melinda explained. "If they're not happy with what they see, they could delay our departure."

"It's almost two thirty. Should we even bother going to the pool? I might just take a walk around the promenade deck. Do you want to come?"

"I think I'll take a nap. Wake me up when you come in. And you should probably plan to be back here by three forty-five."

"Aye, cap," I said, saluting, and stepped out into the hallway.

I did the long trek back to the elevators and waited patiently for a car to arrive. At deck twelve, I discovered a crowd of folks in Bavarian dress — the women in colorful, swirling skirts and the men in lederhosen. I would have asked them who they were, but they appeared to be upset and were complaining in German. I overheard a few words that were the same in both languages: *akkordeon, tuba,* and *trompete.* From the indignation on their faces I gathered they were unable to locate their instruments. I pushed through them and found the door to the outside deck.

The afternoon was heating up, but the city air still harbored a chill. The promenade ran around the circumference of the ship, interrupted here and there with white steel stairways to access the above deck. Every hundred yards or so, several chaise lounges were grouped together for relaxing. I saw a few elderly passengers in wheel chairs already lined up to enjoy the summer afternoon. I smiled hello as I passed.

I completed two trips around the ship before my watch said three thirty, and I headed back inside to prepare for the drill. Already people were clogging the hallways wearing orange life jackets and looking like bewildered sheep. By the time I got back to our stateroom, it was three forty-five, and Melinda had my life jacket waiting.

"Did you get any sleep?" I asked as she helped me into the jacket and hooked up the canvas belts.

"No, Phoebe and Duncan were fighting. Something about her ex-husband. I can't believe I could hear them through these walls. Then there was silence. Hopefully that means they were making up." She winked.

"Reminds me of a college weekend," I said. "And I discovered a German brass band on board. I wonder if we'll get to hear them."

"They might be on the playbill. We'll see. Could be fun. Now grab your ID and let's head for the muster station. Ours is on deck four."

Again, throngs of people, now in orange life jackets, crowded the elevators, making their way to their muster stations. When we got to deck four, it was obvious where we needed to be. There were maybe fifty or sixty folks on the promenade deck just below where three life boats hung suspended on the outside edge of the ship. Young men in crisp white uniforms were calling out stateroom numbers. We waited patiently as they went from 8000 to, ours, 8328.

"Here," Melinda yelled.

Next came 8330. No one answered. The sailor yelled the number again, and again no one answered.

"Say *here*." Melinda poked me.

"Here!" I yelled.

"Where do you think they are?" I asked.

"Still making up, I imagine."

Then Melinda grabbed my arm. "Oh, goodness no. Guess who's here?"

I followed her gaze to a group of men in the back of the crowd.

"The Patriots cap," Melinda said, and I saw a tall man with fair skin and dark hair wearing the red, blue, and gray hat of the Boston football team.

"Who's he?"

"Alastair Oglethorpe," Melinda answered. "Phoebe's ex-husband."

"I guess Phoebe and Duncan saw him too. Hope that's not why they're fighting."

CHAPTER FOUR

DEPARTURE

When Melinda and I returned to our stateroom, we stopped first at the door of 8330 and knocked. There was no answer.

"What should we do?" I whispered.

"Nothing for now, I think," Melinda replied. "Let's ditch these life preservers and get ready for dinner. We're meeting the others for drinks in fifteen minutes."

Unfortunately, our luggage had yet to arrive, so getting ready merely involved a splash of water to our faces and combing our hair.

A few minutes after five, Melinda and I stepped off the elevator onto deck thirteen. The hallway was mostly glass and presented a view of the harbor. Suddenly I felt a jolt and put my arm out to steady myself. The ship was moving.

I glanced up and over at the warehouses and office buildings of New York City that were starting to slide sideways as the ship pulled away from its moorings. I felt a twinge of excitement. My first cruise had officially begun.

"Cool, huh?" Melinda said.

"Let's stay here just a minute," I replied. "I want to watch us leave."

"You stay here; I'll get you a drink. Look, there's two chairs by the glass. What would you like?"

"Vodka martini with a twist of lime."

"Coming up."

As Melinda found an opening in the mob of people at the bar, I sat down on a plush cloth chair and watched the tenements and skyscrapers of Manhattan glide by me. By the time Melinda returned to sit in the companion chair, we were passing the Statue of Liberty. I waved to the statue cheerfully. "See you in ten days," I murmured.

As the statue slipped into the distance I asked, "Everybody in there waiting for us?"

"I didn't see anyone we know," Melinda replied. "Don't worry, we'll catch up with them later. I'm enjoying this too."

We sat in quiet wonder while voices rose and fell behind us like the lapping of the ocean's waves against the ship. I sipped my martini and basked in the joy of the moment. Slowly our ship glided beneath the Verrazano-Narrows Bridge glowing silver in the late afternoon sun. Soon we were out in the cold gray water of the Atlantic Ocean.

"Okay," I finally said when my share of awe was spent. "Let's find the others."

We entered the Art Deco bar and nudged our way through the loud throng, looking for someone we knew. When we got to the far end, we found Rick, Jane, Sylvia, and Liz at a small table against a glass wall. They had obviously been enjoying the view also.

"Hi, guys," Melinda said.

"Where's Phoebe and Duncan?" I asked.

"Don't know," Rick said. "But they missed a hell of a departure."

"They're probably watching it from their balcony," Jane said. "I wouldn't bother them."

Liz spoke up, "Seating for dinner starts at six fifteen. I think we should make our way down to the dining room. I hope they honored our request to sit together."

Everyone stood up. Our small group banded together and began pushing our way through the crowd to the door. We were lucky to find a waiting elevator and descended to deck eleven. As we exited, we saw Phoebe and Duncan, flushed and happy, standing in front of the closed doors to the dining room.

"'Hail, hail, the gang's all here,'" sang Duncan.

As on cue, the double doors swung open, and we descended a short staircase carpeted in a red and blue geometric pattern. I gazed in astonishment at the gleaming marble pillars that supported two upper dining tiers that ringed the main level. On our level, we were surrounded by tables resplendent in white linen and sparkling crystal. The chairs were carved white wood, with seat and back cushions covered in red velvet.

A black-liveried maître d' escorted us to our seats. We were all together, as requested, at a rectangular table adorned with elegant silver place settings and delicately painted china.

Our table was at the back end of the dining room. In the fading light, we could look out over the water at the orange sun falling carelessly into the Manhattan skyline. At the stern of the ship, the churning white water from the engines provided a frothy shelf below the pink and purple clouds

As soon as we were seated, a tall Slavic gentleman in a white server's outfit bowed and introduced himself.

"I am Dmitri," he said. "I will be your waiter in this dining room. I desire only to make you happy. Please view menu while I get your drinks."

Everyone ordered another round, and when the drinks arrived, Rick lifted his martini and said, "A toast to the newlyweds. May they cruise through life as happy as they are today. May the storms be few, the winds gentle, the days warm, and the nights warmer."

We all raised our glasses to our lips. At the same moment, somewhere in the kitchen, a tray of china crashed to the floor. We all shuddered just a bit at the shock of it, but managed to hold onto our glasses. A male voice yelled "*Anak ng puta*," or some such foreign phrase, his anger a rebuke to our happy table. For just a moment, the mood was broken. Then we all remembered that we were toasting the newlyweds and took a sip of our drinks.

Ignoring the resulting commotion that we could overhear thirty yards away, Duncan raised his glass and said, "To my beautiful wife, Phoebe. This is the most joyous day of my life. I hope I can make her half as happy as she has made me."

We all sipped again, gently set down our glasses, and resolutely picked up our menus.

Dmitri appeared like magic to take our orders. We had a choice of two soups, two salads, and three entrees. I chose strawberry soup, spinach salad, and baked chicken. Melinda ordered the vichyssoise, arugula salad, and tilapia.

As we waited and chatted, I noticed how stunning Jane looked in a sunny yellow linen jacket and white shell. Her husband was similarly handsome in a navy blazer and pale blue button-down. They had obviously gotten their luggage. The smiled at each other as they ate, and I was silently pleased to see them getting along so well.

The real surprise was Sylvia, in a black sheath and white pearls that set off her salt-and-pepper hair. The cut and color of her dress took twenty pounds off. I had never seen her look so glamorous.

Maybe she was hoping to meet someone special on this cruise, someone to replace her sad memories with happy ones.

Liz wore an emerald green shell with a short black skirt. Phoebe, Duncan, Melinda, and I were the only ones still dressed in our traveling clothes.

As each course arrived I noted how much smaller these portions were than what you would receive in a stateside restaurant. But when I considered that the dinner had four courses, I decided I was glad that I'd still be hungry enough to enjoy a guilt-free dessert.

The meal was excellent—my chicken was moist without being underdone, Melinda's fish was flaky and mild, and the beef kebobs the others ordered were tender and spicy.

We ate in silence, except for occasional compliments on the deliciousness of our meal. Having spent so much time together earlier in the day, it seemed we had little to say. When we finished, Liz suggested we hurry to make the eight o'clock show in the auditorium. We headed back to the elevators and rode down to deck nine.

The auditorium was another wonder to me, a theater venue as big as any I'd attended on land, with plush chairs ringed around glass tables so that drinks could be served during the show. I was beginning to understand that alcoholic beverages were how cruise ships really made their money.

On stage, the cruise director introduced himself as Sven Angstrom and told us this was International Night. We would be entertained by a German polka band, an Italian opera singer, and finally an Irish traditional group. We all ordered more drinks and grinned drunkenly at each other.

The Germans began with "The Happy Wanderer" polka and got us all clapping to the upbeat brass music and singing "Val-deri," "Val-dera." The Italian tenor changed the pace with love songs to his "Amore." Finally, the Irish band took the stage and had us all laughing with a tale of an ugly hen who was a princess in disguise.

They closed the show with a riotous tune about sailing, drinking, and throwing the first mate overboard. As we tiredly made our way back to our staterooms Duncan was chanting "What shall we do with the drunken matey? Put him in bed with the captain's lady..."

When Melinda and I got to our stateroom, the hallway was littered with our luggage.

I was incredibly tired. Unpacking would have to wait until tomorrow.

CRUISE DAY TWO

MONDAY

CHAPTER FIVE
ILL WINDS

I slept until after nine, a rare occurrence for me because I'm usually up by seven. A glance out the balcony doors partially explained it—sheets of rain fell from dingy clouds.

I also woke up with a slight headache, not a surprise considering all I'd had to drink the day before. As I tottered on unsteady feet to the bathroom, I noticed that Melinda was still asleep. I needed coffee, so I quickly washed my face to remove yesterday's makeup, brushed my teeth, and dressed in yesterday's clothes.

Ready to face the outside, I went to find coffee, guessing I'd find it in the casual dining room where we'd lunched the day before. My watch said nine thirty as I trudged down the long hallway to the elevator.

On deck twelve, energetic couples were power walking in the rain, and I saw a yoga class in session in the workout room.

I grabbed a cup of black coffee and found a chair in a protected area outside where I could sit comfortably and enjoy my daily caffeine fix. I closed my eyes and listened to snippets of conversations from chatty ladies as they passed me on their go-round of the deck. It was warm, maybe seventy degrees, and the rain slowed now to a gentle shower.

Seeing no one I knew, I eventually went back to my stateroom, planning to take a shower and read until Melinda woke up. When I returned, however, I found her in the bathroom, kneeling by the toilet and looking disturbingly pale.

"Are you sick?" I asked, concerned.

"Yes. I don't know whether to suspect the fish, the Norovirus, or too much to drink last night."

"Could you be seasick?"

"I guess that's a possibility too. I have some motion sickness pills in that plastic bag on the shelf. Would you get me one?"

I found the bag and a small tube marked Dramamine™. The directions suggested taking one or two tablets every four to six hours. The package also said to take the tablets one half to one hour before needed. Well, who would know that? I took out two tablets and gave them to Melinda.

"Thank you," she said and popped the pills with water immediately.

"I guess you won't be wanting breakfast?"

"Actually, I think I'd like a cup of tea with lots of sugar."

"You sure that's smart?"

"If not, I'll turn around and come back."

"Do you mind if I shower first?"

"Hurry up," she said, and I did as I was told. In ten minutes I was ready to go. Melinda, meanwhile, washed her face and put on jeans and a sweat shirt.

Like the day before, a uniformed gentleman stood at the entrance of the casual dining room. He had a large squirt bottle of hand sanitizer. We used it and moved on.

When we got a chance to look around the dining room, we found that Phoebe, Liz, and Sylvia were already there, enjoying family-style plates of waffles, eggs, bacon, sausage, fruit, and a selection of Danish.

"You guys went all out," I commented.

"No," Liz said. "The bride went all out. We single ladies still have to watch our figures."

"Not fair," Phoebe replied. "I can't help it if I was born with a fast metabolism."

"But you also get all the men," Sylvia muttered. I almost didn't hear her, but Phoebe clearly did.

"Again, not my fault," she replied. "You were married, Sylvia. I'm sorry you *lost* your husband, but you could still meet someone else and marry again."

For no reason, it struck me as comical the way Phoebe had put emphasis on the word "lost," almost as if Sylvia had misplaced him, like a set of keys. I smiled without thinking.

"Don't smile," Sylvia growled at me. "I bet you don't know that Duncan was dating *me* until I introduced him to Phoebe. Then it was dump-the-fat-lady time."

"And Liz went out with him once, too, about four years ago,"

Phoebe said. "Let's get all the nasty out now so we can move on and enjoy our cruise. Anybody have anything else to add?"

We all looked at Liz for a comment, but she kept her eyes on her bowl of fruit.

"It's just not fair," Sylvia whined. "Phoebe gets all the men, and there's none left over for the rest of us."

"Hey, look at me," Melinda interjected. "I'm single, I have no current boyfriend, and I happen to think I'm pretty hot." She put her right hand on her hip and posed with her left hand behind her raised head. Melinda was six feet tall, with hair that was currently a deep red, and curvaceous hips. She quickly commanded the attention of all those sitting near us.

We silently admired her for two seconds, then she laughed. "And Emily here has been dumped more times than any of you girls," she continued.

My face feigned mock hurt at her words, because I understood what Melinda was trying to do.

The result of her efforts to cajole them out of their bitterness only resulted in their deciding to ignore us and return their attention to breakfast.

I thought I would change the subject.

"What do you do on a cruise ship on a rainy day?"

"Well, there's usually trivia games in the lounges," Jane replied. "In the auditorium there'll be a talk on art, because there's always an art auction near the end of the cruise. There's probably a movie in the afternoon, and then there's my favorite past time...sleep."

"Look at the daily schedule that should have been pushed under your door this morning," Liz said. "It has a list of all the day's activities."

"I didn't see one," I said.

"You can get one on deck nine," Jane advised.

"This afternoon I could get interested in any of those activities Jane mentioned," I said. "For this morning, though, I think I'll just catch up on some reading. I'm still tired from all the stress of getting ready for this trip and yesterday's boarding."

"Let's get my tea," Melinda suggested. The women hadn't offered us any of their food, which would have been more than enough for Melinda and me, so we went off for our own.

"That was ugly," I said to her as I selected a cinnamon raisin bagel, cream cheese, and orange juice. "Does this happen all the time?"

"Sylvia and Liz are not usually so negative, but every few months it seems that they get depressed. Instead of trying to comfort each other, they jointly attack someone else. They'll get over it. They always do."

When we returned to the table, the other women had left so Melinda and I sat down—me to enjoy my breakfast and Melinda to sip her tea.

It seemed like a good time to tell her about the apparition in the porthole I had seen when standing alone on the pier.

"Do you think you saw a ghost?" she asked.

"I'm not sure. It was so vague, and it was daytime. It could have just been a crew member or my imagination."

"Sylvia believes in ghosts."

"Has she ever seen one?"

"I'm not sure. She said something once about seeing her dead husband. She won't talk about it when she's sober. You might try speaking to her sometime when she's been drinking."

"I'll make a point of it...nice to have someone who shares my peculiarity." I wondered if Sylvia had seen the same apparition that I had seen.

"My stomach's feeling much better," Melinda said. "I'm ready for a post-breakfast, pre-lunch nap. What would you like to do?"

"I think I'll read, and maybe, I'll fall asleep too. I could use a completely restful day."

We went back to the stateroom and settled in for the morning. When lunchtime came, it was still raining, so we went up to the casual dining room but didn't see any of our group. I figured the newlyweds wanted to be alone together, and perhaps Jane and Rick were having their own second honeymoon. I could do without listening to Liz and Sylvia complain.

Melinda lunched on crackers and tea while I had a roast beef sandwich. Deciding to grab some more tea to take to our stateroom, Melinda went back to the condiment station. I saw her fill a second cup with hot water, turn, and immediately trip over the feet of the gentleman standing behind her, spilling the hot water directly onto his plaid shorts and bare legs.

"Ow!" he yelled, almost dropping the plate he was balancing in one hand and the tea cup he held in the other.

Melinda's cheeks burst into a scarlet hue.

"I'm so sorry," she said, grabbing napkins and trying to blot up the wet from the hem of his shorts and his thighs. Her actions only resulted in his becoming embarrassed as well, his cheeks flaming a shade to match Melinda's. I was enjoying this scene immensely when I suddenly realized the man was Elvis, the same gentleman Phoebe had fallen against when she tumbled down the stairs yesterday. Poor man!

"Please don't," he said to Melinda. "I'm fine now. It'll dry."

Melinda spoke to him, but I couldn't hear what she was saying. Then they both smiled, and Melinda returned to our table and sat down.

"What was that about?" I asked.

"Lord, I'm so clumsy," she said. "But he's attractive, isn't he?"

I truthfully agreed. He had neatly trimmed white hair and a rugged face that smiled when it wasn't doing anything else.

"I told him I hoped I'd see him again around the ship when one of our party wasn't losing their balance."

"Well, let me know if you change your mind. I think he's *trés beau.*"

"What's with the French?" Melinda asked as I got up to leave.

"I always imagine romantic encounters as sexier when the couple speaks French."

"Get outta here," she replied, blushing again, but smiling.

The afternoon played out pretty much the same as the morning, with my reading and Melinda napping. Sitting on my bed, I could feel the ship's forward motion through the choppy seas, and out the balcony door I could glimpse white-capped waves dancing across the ocean. I watched Melinda nod off and guessed the Dramamine™ had made her drowsy. I was glad to see she had kept down her lunch.

When we met the group in the formal dining room for dinner, everyone seemed to have had a good day. Phoebe and Duncan kept their eyes on each other most of the meal, and even Jane and Rick seemed to be smiling at each other a lot. Liz and Sylvia were quiet. I didn't start any conversations.

After I'd scraped up the last crumb of strawberry cheesecake, Melinda suggested we go to the casino for a few hours. We all agreed that was a good idea.

Once there, I spent most of my time and only a little money playing video poker. I thought I was getting pretty good at it. Each hand I would win just enough to keep the game going for another hand.

The waitress brought me two or three vodka tonics, and the next thing I knew it was ten thirty. I looked around for Melinda and saw her playing roulette with Elvis standing beside her. I silently wished her luck on both gambles. The only other person in sight was Sylvia, busy at one of the slots. I went over to where she sat and noticed two empty wine glasses sitting atop the machine. I thought that was a sign it might be a good time to speak to her about ghosts.

"Winning or losing?" I asked as I sat down in the empty stool next to hers.

"Winning!" she said. "Here comes the waitress. Let's have another drink."

A sultry, dark-eyed young girl stopped before us.

"Another glass of merlot," Sylvia said.

"Vodka and tonic with a twist of lime," I told her, and off she slinked without having said a word.

I started our chat with a safe subject. "Too bad about all this rain. It's not much fun to stay indoors on a cruise."

"I don't mind. I brought my needlepoint and finished two tea towels this afternoon."

"Have you been on a cruise before?"

"Once, with my husband."

"Did your husband enjoy cruising?"

"Oh yes. He introduced me to it. My first cruise was our honeymoon. It was the most wonderful vacation of my life. I have so many photos of it, and every now and then, I'll just blow a whole afternoon pulling out the album, looking at each picture and remembering how happy we were."

The waitress arrived with our drinks and we tipped her a few tokens.

"I'm so sorry you lost him. Can I ask you a very personal question?" I took a gulp of my drink.

Sylvia took a sip of her wine.

"Melinda once told me that when she was little, she had a visit from her grandmother on the night she died. She said the ghost of her grandmother appeared in her room and told her that she was in heaven and Melinda shouldn't worry about her. Then she disappeared. Did your husband ever appear to you after he died?"

"No, I've never actually seen him as a ghost," she said. "But I sort of see him in the sense that I remember what he looked like so intensely that I can picture him with me."

She went on to explain. It would happen unexpectedly, like when she was eating dinner at the kitchen table, and without warning, there he would be, sitting catty-corner to her, facing the little TV on the credenza, watching the evening news.

Or she saw him in a car. If she happened to be riding in the passenger side of someone else's vehicle, she would turn her head toward the driver to say something and there he was again, in profile, his pale moon face fringed with straight blonde hair, his hands on the steering wheel.

Most upsetting of all, she saw him in bed, lying beside her, his big warm body like her own personal mountain, filling up the bed with the warmth of his presence.

She told me that, when the Christmas season came and she neared the one-year anniversary of his death, every day was a heartbreaking milestone of "This time last year he had the chest x-ray" and "On this date last year we were told it was cancer."

Somehow she got through it, every Christmas becoming just slightly easier, every birthday and anniversary a little less upsetting. But the hurt never really went away. When she put flowers on his grave, she would sit on the flat gravestone and talk to him about what was happening in her life and how much she missed him. She said she missed him with an ache the pain of which she'd never thought possible, and she saw no end in sight.

My heart went out to her, and I decided not to ask if she had seen the apparition I had seen.

"I can't imagine surviving a loss like that." I said.

My words startled her out of her reverie. I think she'd forgotten I was there. She had been talking to herself and clinging to her memories of the man she'd loved.

She took another sip of wine and said, "I don't know how I've survived...sheer willpower I guess. Or sheer stupidity."

"It's been a long day," I said to her. "Let me walk you back to your room."

"No, I'd like to stay here a little longer. Please, you don't have to wait for me. Sometimes I like to be alone."

I finished the last of my drink and said, "Okay, I'll see you in the morning."

"I'll follow in fifteen. I still have lots to lose," she joked.

"Good luck," I replied and left. When I got back to our stateroom the bedside clock said eleven thirty. I was asleep before I heard Melinda return.

CRUISE DAY THREE

TUESDAY

CHAPTER SIX

MISSING

Day three, I woke up again at nine. Melinda was still sleeping, so in a repeat of day two, I dressed quietly and went looking for coffee. The rain had cleared up overnight, and the sky was a brilliant blue. I felt the warmth in the soft, southern breeze as I stepped out onto the deck. After finding coffee, I settled in a chair by the pool to enjoy the peaceful morning.

"Emily, you're up." It was Liz, wearing black yoga pants and two different shades of green tee shirts layered on top of each other. "Sylvia's still asleep. Do you know she snores?"

"Oh, I'm sorry to hear that. Did you manage to get any sleep?"

"Yeah, she only woke me up once or twice during the night, and I was able to fall back to sleep each time."

"Want to get some breakfast?"

"No thanks. I've had too much rich food and alcohol these past few days. I need to fast this morning. See you at lunch." Off she went on her power walk.

I was about to get up and head back to the stateroom when Duncan appeared, walking in a jerky, agitated state and glancing all around, staring at everyone.

"Duncan," I called. "How are you?"

He saw me and stopped with a start. "It's Phoebe," he said. "She's missing."

It took me a second to register the importance of what he was saying. Brides don't go missing on their honeymoons. Surely he was mistaken.

"She's probably just having breakfast or walking around the deck," I replied. "Have you looked in the dining rooms?"

"I've looked everywhere...the dining rooms, the decks, the lobby, the shopping areas, the coffee bar. She's not anywhere!"

"How about the yoga class?"

"Checked."

"Maybe she's talking to Sylvia or to Jane and Rick."

"I've woken everyone up...except you and Liz...She was already out...Melinda is dressing...She said she'd come help me look...What should I do?"

Duncan's choppy speech rang with his anxiety. Considering his age, I was worried his agitation would bring on a stroke or a heart attack. He was a very plump man and not in any sort of physical shape to handle extreme stress.

"Sit down, Duncan. Take a breath. I see Melinda coming. We'll find Phoebe."

Melinda didn't look too well herself. She had a yellowish tinge to her face, which was clenched and furrowed.

"Emily, we've got to look for Phoebe. I called Rick, Jane, and Sylvia. They're meeting us in the casual dining room. Sylvia said Liz was gone too."

"Liz is okay. I saw her five minutes ago. She's power walking. I'm sure we'll run into her while we're looking for Phoebe. Here comes everyone else."

Jane and Rick were clutching hands and hurrying as fast as they could. Sylvia was not far behind, walking unsteadily and looking half-asleep.

"Where should we start?" I asked.

Melinda took charge. "Duncan, is there any place you haven't looked?"

"Just the day-care center...and the casino...Phoebe doesn't like to gamble."

"We should check there just to be thorough. Let's break up our search by deck. Jane and Rick, why don't you take deck ten where the stores and casinos are. Duncan, you and Emily double-check your room and take deck nine where the offices and auditoriums are. Sylvia, you search deck eleven where the library and other restaurants are, and I'll double-check this deck, the gym, spa, salon, and the bars on deck thirteen. I know the bars aren't open yet, but I'll look at the lounge areas outside of them. If anyone sees Liz, tell her to join Sylvia. We'll meet at Phoebe and Duncan's room in an hour, and if we still haven't found her we'll alert Security. And don't forget to check all the restrooms, okay?"

"Okay," we said in a chorus.

Melinda had brightened up a bit with the restorative power of positive action. I figured she was pairing me with Duncan because he looked ill and Liz wasn't here to help. I worried a little about Sylvia searching alone, but hopefully she'd soon have Liz to keep her company.

"Let's go back to your room," I said to Duncan as the group broke up to start searching.

We looked in all directions as we made our way back to the elevator. It occurred to me that we could miss her if she was taking an elevator at the same time we were. I had seen at least sixteen elevators in my travels around the ship, but I figured that we could still meet Phoebe at some point.

When Duncan and I got back to his room, we were dismayed to see that Phoebe wasn't there. I went over to the sliding glass door and looked out at an empty balcony.

Duncan sank down wearily on one of the beds, which both appeared to have been slept in. I heard him wheeze as he took a deep breath.

"Do you have asthma, Duncan? Can I get your inhaler?"

"COPD, and yes...yes...look in the bathroom."

I went to the bathroom and found his inhaler. I handed it to him; he took two puffs and seemed to relax. He next managed two shallow breaths with no wheezing. Some color returned to his face.

"Duncan, I think you should stay here in case Phoebe returns. I'll check back in half an hour. If she does return, just wait here for me. Eventually, the rest of group will get the message that Phoebe has been found."

"Where can she be?" he asked.

"I don't know. She might be chatting with the captain in his quarters or inspecting the kitchen. Who knows? There's so many places she could be on a cruise ship. I'm sure she'll turn up."

I left Duncan and took the elevator to deck nine. This was the deck with the business offices and the large show auditorium that we'd been in two nights before. First, I walked the hallways and checked the stalls of all the restrooms. I didn't see anyone. Most people were probably either waking up or getting breakfast.

I didn't think it was appropriate to knock on the office doors at this early stage, so I went to search the auditorium. There, I walked in between each row of seats and even looked down into the orchestra pit. A small set of steps led to each side of the stage.

I walked up to and stood on the stage, examining the view and looking for anyone who might be there. The place was empty.

I peeked backstage, but that entire area was dark. Checking the walls closest to the stage, I couldn't find any light switches, so I called out, "Phoebe, are you here?" No answer.

As I started back down the steps, a voice rang out from above the auditorium in what I guessed was a sound and lighting booth.

"Who's there?" echoed in the vacant room.

"I'm looking for a woman who's gone missing," I called out to the voice.

"I'll be right there," he replied, and as I waited, a tall figure appeared at the back of the auditorium and walked to where I was standing.

"I'm Emily Menotti," I said, introducing myself. The stranger looked familiar.

"I'm Sven, the cruise director."

As soon as he said his name, I recognized him from the first night.

"Did you say someone has gone missing?"

"Yes, Phoebe Blumen. She's traveling with a group of us. Her husband woke up this morning and she was gone. We've been looking for her ever since."

Sven now stood opposite me and I noticed he was not only tall but also had startling green eyes that went well with his salt-and-pepper hair and tan skin. From the crinkles around his eyes and mouth I guessed him to be fifty-five to sixty years old. My age, I noted briefly.

"What's the protocol for someone lost at sea?" I asked.

"If you're sure you can't find her," he said in a soft voice with a Nordic lilt, "you need to speak to Security. What does she look like?"

"Fifties, fair skin, and pale blonde hair. She's very tiny, almost frail."

"She sounds like a fairy child," he said. "I haven't seen any ethereal spirits on board in the five years I've been the cruise director, but I'll keep an eye out for anyone meeting her description. Did you say her name was Phoebe?"

"Yes."

"Married?"

"Yes."

"Husband seem okay?"

"Yes, this is their honeymoon."

"My, my," he commented. "Please let me know if you find her or not. I've got to rush off now to the pool deck to set up for a limbo contest."

"I will," I said, watching him turn and hurry back up the aisle.

I promptly realized that I'd been so distracted by his good looks that I hadn't asked him how to turn on the lights in the backstage area. Well, it was too late now. It would have to wait.

As I left the auditorium, which was at the back of the ship, and passed through the hallways for the offices which were located midships, I came to a second auditorium at the front of the ship. An exact mirror of the other in size and layout, it was decorated in shades of blue and green whereas the other was mauve and gray. White dustcovers were draped across the chairs and tables indicating the room was not in use this trip. I repeated all the steps I had taken to search the first one, including calling out Phoebe's name as I stood at the edge of the backstage area. I wound up with the same results: no Phoebe. No handsome Sven either.

Having done all I could on deck nine, I went back to stateroom 8330. Jane and Rick were already there. Duncan appeared to be calmer.

"Any luck?" I asked.

"No...no luck," Rick said. "You neither?"

Then Melinda arrived, looking ill again. "Did you find her?" I asked, already knowing the answer.

Melinda shook her head and said, "But I did see someone else of interest."

"Who?" we four asked in unison.

"Alastair, Phoebe's ex. It was a little awkward explaining that we couldn't find her and asking him if he'd seen her. He said 'no.' I told him which stateroom we were in and to let us know if he spotted her anywhere."

"How did he seem?"

"Concerned, but that's all. He was in a hurry to meet his girlfriend for breakfast."

Sylvia arrived now, with Liz beside her.

All Sylvia said was "What now?"

"Did anyone check the infirmary?" Melinda asked.

"No," we all again said as one.

"I'll go," I offered.

"I'll go with you," Melinda said. "We can both keep looking while we go there. I think it's all the way down on deck two. The rest of you wait here."

As we walked back along the corridors to the elevators, I asked Melinda if she was okay.

"You look sick," I said. "Did you take any Dramamine™?"

"Yes, I'll be alright. It's something else." Melinda looked around. "I'm feeling that she's not on the ship," she murmured, not wanting to alarm anyone who might overhear us. Being a clairsentient, Melinda could pick up on people's feelings even when they made an effort to mask them.

Melinda and I continued to check off more places to look as the elevator stopped at each deck. Bikini-clad ladies and men in baggy swim shorts entered, pressed their desired floor buttons, and then exited, their carefree banter a discordant soundtrack to our anxiety.

Only Melinda and I were left, along with the lingering scent of coconut oil, when we finally arrived at deck two. We stepped out into a white corridor. We saw yellow and black signs with an arrow and the words "Infirmary/Sykehus" on the steel walls and red footsteps painted on the floor. We followed them and stepped through a doorway into a small, empty waiting room. A freckled, redheaded girl in a white uniform looked up from her desk and asked if she could help us.

"We're looking for our friend Phoebe Blumen, stateroom 8330. Has she been down here?"

"I'll check the log."

She consulted a binder with lined pages on which names and stateroom numbers were written, along with the time of their visit.

"No one with that name or stateroom number," she finally said.

"It might have been last night," I added. "She may have felt sick."

"Oh, okay," she replied and turned back a page.

"Here she is. Yesterday afternoon at four o'clock she came by for seasick pills. We gave her some meclizine and she left," the girl said. Melinda and I looked at each other. That had been the time of the muster station drill; it explained why Phoebe and Duncan hadn't been there.

"Thank you," we both said and turned to leave.

Melinda looked back suddenly and asked, "Would you know if anyone was reported overboard?"

"Did you see something?" the girl asked, voicing alarm. "I haven't heard of anyone."

"No, it's just that we can't find our friend," Melinda explained.

"You should go to Security on deck nine. They would know if anything was reported."

We thanked her again and left.

"Another dead end," Melinda said. "Let's go back and tell the others."

When we returned to the stateroom, Phoebe was still missing. Duncan seemed to be breathing normally, but his eyes were lit up with panic. "Where could she be?" he kept asking.

"Duncan, did anything happen last night that would cause Phoebe to leave your stateroom?" Melinda asked. "Did you guys have a fight?"

"We did have words that first afternoon. On our way back from lunch we ran into Alastair, Phoebe's ex, and he was with a girlfriend. Phoebe was very polite to them, but when we got back to our room, she kept going on and on about how young the girlfriend was and what a lech Alastair was."

He paused to take a deep breath and continued, "I could tell she was jealous. I got angry and said that she obviously still cared for him."

He stopped again to get his breath. "It took a while for me to calm her down. Then she started to feel seasick, and we went to the infirmary on deck two for pills. She recovered pretty quickly, and she seemed fine at dinner. You saw her. We had a nice time at the show. We were both tired afterward and went to sleep right away."

"And yesterday?"

"Everything was good. We mostly slept in the morning and went to the movie in the afternoon. You saw us at dinner. We were fine."

"Did either of you go out on the balcony last night?" I asked.

"Just briefly...to see the moonlight. The rain had cleared and there was a full moon. Then we went to bed."

I glanced out at the balcony and saw that the chairs and table had been moved from their earlier position to a spot against the side of the ship. A person would have had to climb onto the table to get over the railing. Would Duncan have had any reason to push Phoebe overboard? I didn't know Duncan very well, but the others seemed to accept what he said as the truth.

"Let's establish a time line," I suggested. "Duncan, when exactly was the last time you saw Phoebe?"

"Eleven o'clock last night. That's about the time we went to bed."

"And what time did you wake up this morning?"

"Around nine."

"Are her night clothes here or did she get dressed before she left?"

"Oh, I didn't think of that," he said. We glanced around. No nightgown or bathrobe was in sight. I walked over to the bathroom and looked behind the door. Nothing hanging there either.

"Do you mind if I look in the drawers?" I asked.

"No, of course not."

"Oh," Duncan hesitated. "I remember now...when we went to bed, she wasn't wearing anything." His cheeks went pink as he said this.

Melinda helped me check each drawer. There were only six of them: three filled with men's underwear, tee shirts, and socks and three with Phoebe's undergarments and two sweaters. There were also two satin negligees, one white and one lavender. They didn't look as if they'd been worn. We also checked the tiny closet where Phoebe had hung shorts, dresses, and knit tops.

"Time to go to Security," Melinda said. "I'll go with Duncan. They'll want to speak to the husband. The rest of you can do as you like...stay here or search the ship again. Just let us know if Phoebe returns. Duncan, we'll need a photo. Do you have one?"

"Uh...no," he said. "We didn't bring any photos with us. We were planning to take a bunch, though."

"Is Phoebe's ID card here? I mean the one she got when you boarded the ship."

"No, I already looked. She must have it with her."

"Okay, the ship will have a copy of it."

The two of them left, Duncan with his head hanging down and shuffling his feet. I looked around at the others. "I'd like to walk the ship again. Anyone want to join me?"

"I will," Liz offered.

"We'll look some more too," Rick said, nodding at his wife.

"I guess I'll stay here then," Sylvia said.

Liz and I left the stateroom and I asked her where she thought we should start.

"You know her better than I do," I explained. "What were her hobbies? What would she be interested in?"

"She loves to read, so let's check the library again."

"The bars will be open now too," I said. "We can speak to the bartenders."

We took the elevator to deck eleven and made a quick search of the library. Next, we went up to deck twelve and checked out the spa and salon, with no luck.

"Do you have any theories?" I asked Liz as we searched.

"My guess is that she became ill, or maybe she was seasick again, or maybe she had too much to drink. And there's the Norovirus. Maybe she caught that, and she leaned over the railing to throw up. She could have lost her balance and fallen overboard."

"The infirmary said she had asked for seasick pills, and she didn't seem drunk or ill at dinner."

"No, but that Norovirus hits hard, out of the blue. Or maybe she couldn't sleep and went out for a nightcap."

When we reached deck thirteen, it was almost noon and the doors to the specialty bars were open. A few folks were already seated on the bar stools enjoying a Bloody Mary. We started at the Art Deco bar and approached the bartender, a muscular young man with olive skin and short black curls. Michelangelo's *David* crossed my mind.

"Were you here tending bar last night?" I asked him.

"Yes," he replied in a thick Mediterranean accent.

"Did you see a fiftyish woman in here late last night? Very tiny and blonde."

"No, ma'am," he said, and that was all. I wondered if he even understood English other than drink orders and minimal phrases for polite conversation about the ship.

These questions and the same answers were repeated at the Old English pub and the jazz club. At the disco bar, the bartender, another young man of Mediterranean background, seemed hesitant, but at least, he spoke English.

"There was a group of older women in here late last night. I'm not sure if one of them was the woman you're looking for. They looked a lot like you ladies."

"Were they American?" I asked.

"I couldn't tell. The waitress took their orders."

"Do you remember anything else about them? Did you overhear what they were talking about?" Liz asked.

"No, I'm sorry. That's all I know."

"When will the waitress be on duty?" I asked.

"Three o'clock."

"Okay, we'll come back," I told him. Liz and I left.

"Let's just check the pool area one more time," Liz suggested as we left the bar. "Phoebe loves to sit in the sun and read."

On deck twelve, the pool was mobbed with sunbathers; not an empty chair was to be found. We zigzagged in between the lounge chairs. The small tables in between them were already crowded with plastic tumblers of beer and frothy pink drinks.

The ship suddenly shivered and came to a halt. A squawk from the loudspeakers reverberated around the deck. Immediately, we heard the captain's voice. Liz and I stopped to listen.

"Good morning, passengers," he began. "This is Captain Bonaparte. We are enjoying beautiful weather, and I hope you are making use of the pool and the other forms of recreation that can be found on board the *Galleon of the Galaxy*. However, it is necessary to delay our voyage briefly while we locate a Mrs. Phoebe Blumen. If she is hearing my voice, please report to the Security Office on deck nine. It is most urgent that we speak with you. This has been your captain speaking."

A tall man suddenly stood up and looked around. I recognized him; he was Alastair, Phoebe's ex. Liz saw him too and waved. He weaved his way through the lounge chairs to join us.

"Is it true?" he said to Liz. "Phoebe really is missing? I didn't quite believe Melinda this morning. I figured Phoebe would have turned up by now."

"Yes, she disappeared from her stateroom last night. Are you sure you haven't seen her?" Liz asked.

"Why would I have seen her?"

"I don't know," Liz said, annoyed at his question. "Maybe you were out late and saw her on deck somewhere or in one of the bars."

"No! Of course, I didn't see her."

"Were you in any of the bars late last night?" I asked. Alastair gave Liz a look that plainly said, "Who the hell is this?"

She picked up on it and introduced me, "This is Emily. Emily, this is Alastair. Emily's helping me look for Phoebe." Then Liz turned to me and added, "He and Phoebe were married for twenty years, until Alastair got itchy."

"That's not fair," he responded angrily. "The decision to split was mutual."

"Right," Liz muttered. "Is that why you hired a lawyer and fought paying alimony? I'm glad Phoebe won that one, although I guess you're off the hook now that she's remarried."

"As a matter of fact, I'm not off the hook. I'm suing my lawyer for malpractice. When he wrote up the separation agreement, he forgot to include a clause saying the alimony would end when Phoebe remarried. I assumed the definition of alimony meant payment to an unmarried person, and that it would automatically end when she got hitched. But, big frigging surprise, in my case it doesn't."

"Whoa..." I interjected. "This isn't helping us find Phoebe. Please, Alastair, think back on last night. When you were in and out of the bars, you didn't see Phoebe anywhere?"

"No, I didn't, and we were in and out of most of them. My girlfriend and I decided to have a drink in each one to celebrate our vacation."

"From when to when?" I asked.

"Approximately ten to midnight."

"Please let us know if you do see her," I said. "I'm in stateroom 8328."

"I will," he said and, with a glare at Liz, turned and stomped off.

"I'm guessing Phoebe is better off without him," I said.

"Yes, we were all agreed on that one. Let's head back to the room and see if she's shown up."

Everyone was there: Sylvia, Jane and Rick back from searching, and Duncan and Melinda back from Security. Only Phoebe was missing.

"We heard the captain's announcement," I said. "What else can he do?"

"They're going to lower some of the lifeboats down into the water and take a look at the ship from the outside," Melinda replied. "They'll examine it for any signs that someone went overboard, and the Security staff will search every square inch of the ship."

"What can *we* do now?" Duncan asked, looking paler than before.

"Let's put together some scenarios that might explain what Phoebe did last night," I suggested. "Who wants to start?"

"I'll start," said Duncan. "We went to sleep around eleven, so I'm going to guess that she woke up later during the night and either needed to use the bathroom, or was hungry and went looking for something to eat."

"Would she have gone out on the balcony to look at the moonlight?" Melinda asked.

"Yes, she could have done that also," Duncan replied.

"Going out to the balcony or going to the bathroom doesn't explain why she wasn't in the room this morning." I said.

"She could have gone out to the balcony and then felt ill," Liz responded. "If she leaned over the railing to throw up, she could have fallen overboard." I noted that this was the second time Liz had suggested this scenario.

"Could she have dropped something off the balcony and gone to reach for it and fallen overboard?" Rick asked.

"Wait, aren't there video surveillance cameras?" Jane asked.

"The captain said there were, and he would get to back to us as soon as he'd reviewed them," Melinda answered.

"It could take all day," Duncan said.

"What other explanations are there?" Rick asked.

"What about her going for something to eat?" Jane suggested. "The casual dining room always has a small selection of snack foods available, even in the middle of the night. I think there was also a midnight buffet in the pool area last night. They have midnight buffets most nights."

"Maybe we could ask the staff," Melinda suggested. "But we'll need to wait until the night crew comes on duty."

"Let's hope we've found her by then," Jane said.

"How about if she went out looking for food and passed out somewhere?" Melinda said. "Duncan, I'm guessing you couldn't tell us if she packed a particular outfit and it's missing now?"

Duncan shook his head. "I've no idea what she packed or what's missing." This didn't strike me as odd but as typically male. No one else objected to it either.

"I'm embarrassed to say this, but I'm very hungry," Jane broke in. "Would it be okay if we continued this discussion over some food?"

"Yes! I'm famished," Rick responded, nodding to Jane.

"Not me," Duncan panted. "I'm not feeling well."

"You guys go," I said. "I'll stay with Duncan. Just bring me back a turkey sandwich. In fact, double that order. Maybe you'll eat something, Duncan?"

"I'll try."

They left, leaving Duncan and me alone.

"Where's that note you guys got with your flower arrangement yesterday?" I asked Duncan.

"Over there, next to the TV."
I found it and read it again:

Fair of skin is not pure of heart
Blue eyes see little in the dark
When blood turns black and eyes burn green
Beware the secrets now unseen.

I was willing to bet whoever wrote those words knew exactly what had happened to Phoebe.

CHAPTER SEVEN

SYKEHUS

Duncan squirmed on his bed and reached for his inhaler. I busied myself with straightening up the other bed where the women had sat. I thought it odd that the two single beds were still separated. Phoebe and Duncan hadn't moved them together as I would have done if I were on my honeymoon with my new spouse. But who knew what their reasons might be? Perhaps one had a snoring problem, or they'd just been too tired these last two nights to bother, or maybe the beds were too heavy to move.

The inhaler no longer seemed to be helping Duncan; his breathing grew raspier, more a wheeze than a breath.

"It's too bad the Security folks weren't more forthcoming with plans and procedures," I said to him. "But, I'm sure they'll search everywhere."

"Yes, but they said they would do it very discreetly; they didn't want the other passengers alarmed. I can't say that I care much whether the passengers are alarmed or not. Maybe one of them saw something helpful."

"And they're reviewing the camera footage?"

"Yes."

"I guess there's not too much else that they can do."

"They can investigate me, and that's probably what they're doing right now."

"What do you mean?"

"They wanted to know if I'd taken out any insurance policies on Phoebe recently. I told them that, of course, I had. I took out both medical and life insurance through the travel insurance agency on their website.

"Let's face it," he continued, the timbre of his voice worrying me. "I have health problems. I was really thinking of those funds taking care of Phoebe if anything should happen to *me*. I'm not sure the Security folks saw it that way. Maybe they think I'm guilty of fraud."

His effort at conversation had upset Duncan even further. Perspiration was beading up on his forehead and sliding down his face. He dabbed at the moisture with a Kleenex.

"Do you have any other medicines to help you breathe?" I asked.

"No," he replied and choked on his own breath.

"Maybe you and I should go down to the infirmary," I said. "They might have something to help you."

He nodded "Yes" rather than spoke.

I wrote a note for the others and, folding it, I inserted it between the door and the doorjamb to prevent the door locking. The others would be able to get in, or Phoebe could read it and know where we were.

When we got to the elevators, the German band was again commandeering all the available cars. I spoke to the gentleman with the tuba. "Please, my friend needs to get to the infirmary. Can we go ahead?"

He shook his head "no," and I wasn't sure if that meant "No, I don't speak English," or "No, I won't give up my place in the elevator."

I looked in panic at the other band members filling the hallway: two men holding clarinets, one woman with a trombone, and a man with an accordion. Perhaps they could see the fear in my eyes or that Duncan was struggling to breathe, because after a few moments, the woman took the tuba player's arm and said something in German.

"*Ja*," he said.

At that moment an elevator arrived, and the band took a step back so Duncan and I could enter. I was so relieved that I didn't have to create a scene to get Duncan into that car.

The exertion of walking down the long hallway to the elevator had taken its toll on Duncan. He leaned back against the wall of the car and closed his eyes. His chest was heaving with the effort to suck in additional air. I was panicking with worries that the elevator could stop working. What would we do then?

Slowly, so slowly, the elevator made its descent and, luckily, made no other stops. At deck two, Duncan staggered out of the car, and I guided him over the painted footsteps to the infirmary.

Seeing Duncan's distress, the girl at the desk immediately

jumped up to help me support Duncan's weight as we guided him to a chair. "Wait here," she said and disappeared into the office.

Within five seconds a young Asian doctor appeared. She was tiny, maybe five feet tall, and looked way too young to be a doctor. I wondered if this was her first job out of med school. I hoped not.

"Let's take him in the back," she said in English, and again, I was grateful; at least language wouldn't be an issue. The receptionist and I helped Duncan up and through the doorway to an examination room. The doctor quickly produced a mask and a green canister of oxygen. Duncan grabbed for the mask and pressed it to his face.

"What happened?" she asked me. Before I could answer, she added, "Are you his wife?"

"His wife is missing and we can't find her," I explained. "I don't know this man very well; he's a friend of a friend. I was staying with him while the others are searching for his wife. He's very upset, and it seems to have triggered some kind of an attack."

I looked over at Duncan who was making a miraculous recovery with the oxygen. His breathing was slower and deeper. He had stopped sweating. I felt my own panic subside.

"What medications is he taking?" she asked me.

"I'm sorry. I don't know."

Duncan raised his arm to get our attention. Then he reached into his pocket and brought out his wallet. From there he extracted a list and handed it the doctor.

"Have you missed taking any of these?" she asked.

Duncan pulled the mask from his face. "I haven't had any furosemide since we left port. I'm sure I packed it, but I can't find it."

The doctor turned and looked at me accusingly as if this was all my fault. "Why didn't you come down here sooner?"

"We've been too busy looking for his wife," I answered.

"I don't mean that," she barked. She turned to Duncan. "You should have been down here the very first day and told me you didn't have your diuretic. I could have given you some. Now I don't know how much damage you've done to yourself."

So much for bedside manner, I thought. She turned to me again.

"What's wrong with you old people signing up for cruises when you have health issues? I don't have the resources to deal with these kinds of problems. We're two days from port and another full day and night to St. Thomas. What am I going to do with him?"

I wanted to slap her. Who did she think went on cruises—healthy twenty-somethings who would rather be rock climbing or skydiving? We "old people" were her bread and butter. She had some nerve to speak to us like that. It wasn't her job to judge—it was her job to help. I didn't trust myself to open my mouth in Duncan's defense.

Duncan hung his head, ashamed and sad. I felt sorry for him. What should have been a happy honeymoon cruise had turned into a nightmare. The only thing that would help would be if we found Phoebe alive and well.

An awkward sixty seconds of silence followed as the doctor busied herself taking Duncan's temperature and blood pressure.

"I'll have to keep him here," the doctor finally said. "I'll give him furosemide and then treat him with the nebulizer to clear his lungs. Please give my assistant his name and room number, then bring me his other medications. I'll need to speak to the captain about his prognosis. I don't think we can turn around now and go back to New York. If he doesn't improve, we'll have to send him to the hospital in St. Thomas."

I smiled a half-sad, half-hopeful good-bye to Duncan. Stopping at the desk in the waiting room, I gave the receptionist Duncan's full name and room number. Then I left.

When I got back to the room, everyone was there. Hungry, I was happy to see the turkey sandwiches on the table and grabbed one. I'd take Duncan's food and meds down to him when I finished.

"Duncan is staying in the infirmary," I told them, in between bites. "He lost or forgot to pack one of his meds, a diuretic, and that's complicating his breathing problem. The doctor was pretty nasty to us," and I repeated the conversation along with my thoughts about her attitude.

"Where do these cruise doctors come from?" Rick asked.

"Seems like a cushy job to me," Sylvia said.

"If she has to take care of Duncan for two days until we get to St. Thomas, I don't envy her." Liz said. "I'm thinking she doesn't have the best equipment down there."

The loudspeaker suddenly squawked to life.

"This is Captain Bonaparte with an urgent message to our passengers. If there is a respiratory therapist on board, would you please report to the infirmary? We have a passenger in need of treatment. Thank you."

The message was short and to the point, an indication of the urgency of the situation. Obviously Duncan was not improving as much as I thought he was.

As the captain talked, the ship started moving again. We all looked at each other. "I guess they didn't find anything in the water or outside the ship," Melinda said.

Unexpectedly, the phone rang and she answered, "Room 8330."

Melinda spoke little but appeared to be listening intensely. After she said, "Thank you," she put down the receiver and turned to us.

"That was Security. They couldn't find anything outside and they haven't found Phoebe anywhere inside the ship. They want us in their office at four o'clock to discuss the situation."

"This is it," Jane said. "She's still missing...and...maybe she's dead."

We sat there stunned for a moment, each processing this new information. My own thoughts were that, now, we were searching for a body. Phoebe had obviously met with foul play and her remains had been hidden away or tossed overboard. She wasn't my good friend, though, so I felt it was wrong to voice my opinion in front of these women who obviously knew her so much better than I and would feel her loss deeply.

"I have to round up Duncan's meds," I reminded them.

Locating his white plastic box for his daily meds and the appropriate pill bottles was a welcome distraction for a few minutes. I found a gallon plastic bag in the bathroom with six bottles. I glanced at them quickly. I wasn't familiar with all of them, but I did recognize the low-dose baby aspirin; the propranolol, a popular heartburn medication; and another pill for high cholesterol. I also saw a bottle labeled Viagra™. I took that bottle out and put it back in the bathroom. He certainly wasn't going to need it in the infirmary.

I went back into his bureau drawers and brought out two pairs of jockey shorts and two white tees. I looked around and saw a few books and magazines and put them with the underwear in a bag. I included a recent Stephen King novel with a bookmark which suggested this was his current read. Perhaps this fictional horror story would divert his attention from the real-life one he was living.

I looked around at everyone else. They were seated on the two single beds looking glum and at a loss for what to do next. I think we were all feeling overwhelmed. We had a missing bride, a very ill groom, a strange environment with unknown rules and protocols, and no one with experience in these situations to guide the way.

"Will you all be here when I get back?" I asked.

"It's three thirty now," Melinda said. "If we're not here, come down to Security. Our meeting's at four. I hope they have something positive to tell us."

I left them looking sad and hopeless. I was glad to have something to do.

In the middle of the afternoon, few people walked the hallways, and I made it down to the infirmary with no delays. When I walked into the waiting room, I spoke to the receptionist.

"I have Duncan Blumen's medications and a change of underwear, along with some lunch. Can I take these back to him?"

"No, I'm sorry, you can't. He's with the respiratory therapist right now. They're trying to keep him breathing. Your friend is in very bad shape."

Tears sprung to my eyes, even though I barely knew Duncan. His wife was missing, and he was fighting for his life. Could a vacation possibly go more wrong?

"I'll check back later," I said, leaving my bundle on her desk.

As I returned to room 8330, I could sense the ship moving forward at a fast clip. It was a truly odd experience, as if our little microcosm of passengers and crew were being forcibly driven into the future. I felt like I was trapped in Dr. Who's TARDIS hurtling through space. We had been stopped for a few hours while they looked for Phoebe, now the captain was trying to make up for lost time.

The stateroom was empty, so I went to Security. The woman at the desk ushered me into a small conference room. The captain himself sat at the head of the dark, highly polished table. As I found myself a chair, I caught his words, "There is nothing more we can do."

"I'm sorry to be late," I apologized and quickly asked, "You searched the ship and found nothing?"

"We couldn't find her," he said.

"Did you search the decks that we couldn't access? Decks one and three?"

"I said," he repeated with an unkind glare directed at me, "that we didn't find her. In addition, you missed what I was telling your friends before your arrival. I explained that we looked at relevant video footage near all of your staterooms and decks twelve and thirteen. One of the video cameras caught a flash of something falling from the balcony of cabin 8103 on our first night out. That's the stateroom of your friends Sylvia Marsh and Liz Spode. It was too small to make out what it was. It could have come from a higher deck, and it wasn't large enough to be a person. It's most likely a cigarette butt." We looked at each other briefly, acknowledging that none of us smoked.

No one else speculated on what the item might be.

"Then last night," he continued, "our cameras caught other mysterious items going overboard during the night. On the starboard side, something shiny was thrown from deck thirteen at approximately 12:35 a.m."

"Could you tell what it was?" I interrupted.

"No, it was too small, maybe a piece of silverware or foil. Because of all the drinking on that deck, we see all kinds of things go over the railing."

He continued, "Ten minutes later, on the same side, something also appeared to go overboard from deck twelve. Although these images aren't especially clear...in fact, they're quite blurry...it didn't look like a person. Very often what we capture is the result of someone leaning over the railing and being ill. Deck twelve, as you know, houses the casual dining room. Someone could have been eating and thrown away a paper plate or cup. This happens all the time on cruises. People are very inconsiderate."

He said all this with a tight smile of superiority on his taut, tan face, peering at us with little slits for eyes, as he passed judgment on us and our activities. We were all, his look and manner said, being "very inconsiderate."

"What were people in the videos doing when these things went overboard?" I asked.

"Just milling around, looking at the ground, searching for something. Nothing suspicious."

"Phoebe was tiny," Jane spoke up, ignoring the implied slight. "She might not look like much on a video camera."

"Did you question anyone?" I asked. I didn't care if these concerns had already been covered before I arrived. In moments of stress we retain very little of what we're told. A repeat of the facts would be helpful for everyone, and I certainly didn't care about inconveniencing this captain.

"My Security team questioned all the staff at meetings this afternoon. No one recalled seeing your friend, or anything unusual."

"Did any passengers report seeing anything odd?" I pressed on.

"The passengers have not been questioned, but I'm sure if someone had seen anything suspicious it would have been conveyed to one of my staff. You should know that we are also looking into the life insurance that Mr. Blumen took out on his wife. It was not a large sum, but it's an angle we must pursue."

"Believe me," Liz spoke up, "I know Duncan. He has no need to murder his wife for a paltry five or ten thousand dollars."

"It still needs investigating," the captain replied. "I'm very sorry, but there is nothing more I can do until we get to St. Thomas. I will file a report with the harbormaster there and with my superiors.

"My understanding," he continued, "is that we might also be transferring Mr. Blumen to the hospital on St. Thomas. Our travel coordinator will contact his family and make arrangements for the Blumens' luggage. You may want to discuss among yourselves if one of you might want to stay with him. The travel coordinator can also find you a room."

The captain nodded to a sleek-haired young woman sitting next to him also in a stiff white uniform. Her face was pale and showed no emotion whatsoever. "Miss Carlisle will be your contact for any questions or concerns while you are still aboard the ship. She will give you her personal extension. Are there any more questions for me?"

I looked around at the stunned faces of my friends. We couldn't ask the questions we wanted to ask, such as "How does such an awful thing happen to a wonderful couple just starting their life together?" Or "How do we tell her children?" Or "When will this nightmare be over?"

"What should we do next?" Rick had the presence of mind to ask.

"There's not much you can do," Miss Carlisle replied, signaling that she was now our resource. "Mr. Blumen is too ill for visitors. All I can suggest is that you try to relax and enjoy the amenities on board. We'll be in St. Thomas the day after tomorrow. From there, you can decide whether to continue on with your cruise or make arrangements to return home."

Was she suggesting that they wanted us off the ship?

She matter-of-factly handed us each a business card with her name and phone number.

We silently stood up and made our way toward the door.

"We'll let you know if anything else develops," Miss Carlisle said as we filed out into the hall.

No one responded; we were too depressed.

Perhaps I was inexperienced in dealing with personal tragedies that happened in a foreign environment, but I would have given good money for some Southern charm and empathy. I was reminded of Dolly Parton's character in *Steel Magnolias*. I wanted someone with a few ounces of human kindness to hold our hands and tell us how sorry they were for our plight, that they understood our heartbreak, and that everything possible was being done to resolve Phoebe's disappearance and Duncan's ill health. Was it the foreignness of our hosts or simply corporate coldness that left us feeling so abandoned in our ordeal?

Dinner was a somber affair. It was formal night, and although we were all decked out in our finest, with Rick in his black and white tuxedo looking like an extra in a James Bond movie, and even Melinda cleaning up nicely in a startling red, off-the-shoulder satin gown, we rarely talked and smiled even less.

"No happy tonight?" Dmitri asked.

"Our friend Phoebe is missing and her husband is in the infirmary. We don't have much to be happy about tonight," Jane spoke for us all.

"Yes, I heard," he replied. "Very sad. I will ask around my friends. Maybe someone see her. She was small, yellow-haired woman, correct?"

"Yes," Jane said. "We're in cabin 8101 if you hear anything. And Emily and Melinda are in 8328. We're afraid she went overboard."

"It happens," he said somberly. "But I will help. I will ask all the night staff in the dining room and the bars if they saw her. Maybe I will have news, no?"

"We hope so," Melinda said.

After dinner and changing into regular clothes, we went down to the infirmary to see Duncan despite the captain's admonishment not to. The doctor was not in evidence and the receptionist waved us through.

He seemed much better. He had oxygen tubes tucked into his nasal passages, and he didn't seem to be in any physical distress. We had interrupted his reading of the Stephen King novel.

A tray with a half-eaten breast of chicken, some mashed potatoes, and green beans sat on the tray table that had been pushed to the bottom of the bed.

"No news?" he asked when he saw us.

"I'm afraid not," Sylvia said. She took his left hand and squeezed it gently. "How are you feeling now?"

"I'm doing much better. The doctor gave me some furosemide. The bottle was missing from my bag of pills. I must have somehow forgotten to pack it, but I'm sure I had it when I left home. Anyway, she can give me medication until we reach St. Thomas. Then I'll probably be transferred to the hospital. She says I'm too sick to continue on the cruise."

"Oh Duncan, I'm so sorry this has happened," Sylvia purred. Her tone belied her words, however. Her soothing words sounded less than sincere. "And has there been any word about Phoebe?" she asked, cradling his left hand in both of hers.

"The captain has spoken to me," Duncan replied. "When we reach St. Thomas, he'll file a missing person's report. All the ships in the area have been alerted to look out for anything floating in the water that might be a body. But he wasn't too hopeful. What am I going to tell her children?"

His good mood immediately vanished. He eyes became damp, and he looked down at his lap.

"And what about *your* children?" Jane asked. "Can one of them come to St. Thomas? Or would you like someone to stay with you? I don't think you should be there alone."

"No, no, that won't be necessary. I've already spoken to my son, Justin, and told him everything that's happened. He'll fly in to meet me. I just can't believe this has happened. How could it have happened? Phoebe would never do anything foolish." He looked down at his lap again.

A tear spilled from the corner of one eye, and I found myself worrying that his emotional state would affect his recovery. However, we could do nothing but reassure him that she would be found.

"Please be optimistic," Jane said. "Even our waiter, Dmitri, is going to ask around the staff to see if anyone saw or heard anything last night. Maybe he'll learn something useful."

Before he could reply a nurse came in, saying "Visiting time is up."

As we walked to the elevators, Melinda said, "I feel so sorry for him. His wife is missing, and he can't help look for her."

"I don't feel sorry for him," Liz responded. "This is what happens when you smoke cigarettes for most of your life."

"But I thought he quit years ago," Melinda said.

"Doesn't matter. By the time you're thirty-five or forty, your fate is sealed. He's just getting what he deserves."

I looked at Liz in horror, but said nothing. I didn't want to start an argument. No one else spoke either, probably for the same reason. Not even Sylvia rose to Duncan's defense.

We took the elevator to deck ten and wandered back to the casino where we sat and drank rather than return to our cheerless rooms. We lamented that the day's activities had shed no further light on what had transpired. We still had no idea of what happened to Phoebe.

Elvis appeared and said "Hello" to us all and directly turned to Melinda. "Would you like to go over to one of the lounges for a drink?" he asked her.

"I'd love to," she said and glanced at me quickly. I smiled an approval. I don't think Melinda had been on a date in over a year. I watched them walk off and admired the way Elvis took her left hand and set it in the crook of his right arm. *Quite the gentleman,* I thought.

After they left, I sat staring into my vodka and tonic, when a tall woman in the peasant garb of the German band approached me.

"The missing woman, she was your friend, *ja?*" she asked.

"Yes," I said.

"Everybody on ship is talking about her. I saw her, last night, in the disco bar on deck thirteen. She was dancing, but I couldn't see who she was with...maybe just a bunch of people all dancing together. She seemed tipsy."

"What time was this?" I asked.

"Did you tell the captain?" Rick interrupted.

"*Ja,* I told the captain. It was maybe eleven thirty or twelve. I can't be sure. I was tipsy too."

"When did you tell him?" I asked.

"Right after I heard him on the loudspeaker."

"I wonder why he didn't mention it to us." Rick said. "He hasn't been very helpful."

"Did anyone else in your party see anything?" I asked.

"No, I'm sorry. Just me. I hope they find your friend."

"Thank you for talking to us," I said, nodding.

"No problem," she said and left.

"So she definitely was out of their room!" Jane shouted in

disbelief. People turned to look at us for a moment and rapidly dismissed us. "Who was she with?" Her questioning eyes stopped at each of us briefly. "Who was dancing with her?"

After a short silence Rick coughed and said, "I was."

In the shocked silence that followed, the question immediately seared my brain: *Why hadn't he told us?*

All eyes turned to Rick, and Jane's were not kind.

"You? Why would you go dancing with Phoebe?" Jane cried out. Rick flinched as if hit by gunfire. Jane went on, "Since when do you go dancing in the middle of the night with someone not your wife?"

"You don't like to dance," Rick pouted. At once, he realized we were all glaring at him. "I didn't set out to go dancing. After you went to sleep, I couldn't settle down so I thought I'd go out and get a drink. I went to the disco bar and there was Phoebe, doing the Twist in the middle of a group of young men, none of whom looked American. I was worried they would take advantage of her, so I went over and told them to leave, that I was her dancing partner. She didn't object. She just blew kisses at them as they left."

"She was drunk," Sylvia said.

"Well, we all knew she liked to drink," Liz said. "And Duncan's not healthy enough to dance. I've often thought she just married him for his money."

"Hey!" The cry erupted from Jane. "Let's not dis her when she's not around to defend herself. I never thought she married Duncan for his money. They seemed genuinely in love."

"It doesn't hurt that he's loaded," Liz said.

"I think half his salary goes to alimony," said Sylvia.

"She's dated men wealthier than Duncan," Jane countered. "If it was just money she wanted, she could have married one of them."

I was very uncomfortable. I didn't know these people well at all, and it saddened me that the stress of the situation was bringing out the worst in them.

"What happened after you danced with her, Rick?" I asked.

"She talked about Duncan...I think she really does love him... She just couldn't sleep. The band was good, and we danced some more. After fifteen or twenty minutes I told her I was tired and suggested I walk her back to her stateroom. She said she wasn't tired and would have one more drink and then go back to Duncan."

"What time was this?" I asked.

"I'm not sure. Maybe between twelve and twelve-fifteen."

"Why didn't you stay with her?" I asked.

"I thought the ship was safe. I didn't know she was going to go missing."

"Why didn't you tell us right away?" Jane asked, hurt and confusion in her voice.

"Well, I knew you'd be angry, and I don't see how it helps explain what happened to her."

"But you should have made sure she returned to her stateroom safely," I responded.

"Look, I don't see myself as the bad guy here. I rescued her from those foreigners. End of story."

It wasn't the end of the story for the rest of us. I could guess that we were all thinking the same thing: that Rick was the last one of us to see Phoebe alive.

Not wanting to be in the middle of a domestic squabble, I said "I'm going to bed" and got up to leave.

When I got back to our stateroom, I found a book to read as I waited for Melinda to return.

After an hour, she appeared.

"How'd it go?" I asked as she changed into pajamas.

"He's from Wilmington, Delaware," she said. "Your hometown. I asked him if he knew you, but he didn't. He works for the DuPont Company as a research scientist."

"It's either chemicals or banking in Wilmington," I said. "I was in banking. So...Do you like him?"

"Yes, but I think I've got lots of competition on board. I'm trying not to get my hopes up."

"What more could he ask for? You've got beauty *and* brains. I hope he's smart enough to realize that."

"Thanks. So what did you guys talk about after I left?"

I told her about Phoebe dancing with the foreign gentlemen and, soon after, Rick dancing with Phoebe.

"He claims he left her there alone. What a rat. He should have stayed with her. What if those gentlemen came back and took advantage of her?"

"I agree. So that makes him the last one of us to see her. Hmmm..."

"You know them better than I. Was there ever anything going on with those two? Can you think of a motive for him to want to hurt her?"

"Phoebe and Rick dated in high school, but that's ancient history," she replied.

"When Phoebe and Alastair divorced, did Rick act like he might be interested in her again?" I asked.

"No, I don't remember Rick being overly friendly or solicitous. I don't think he'd make a move on Phoebe. However, considering the fact that Phoebe seems to have had a lot to drink last night, anything could have happened."

I could see Melinda thinking about Phoebe and Rick.

"Oh, I just remembered something else, but it happened too long ago to matter," she continued.

"What?"

"Way back, when Jane and Rick were first married, Phoebe and Alastair were visiting them, and it was snowy and icy outside. I don't recall the details, but Phoebe was walking to the car and slipped on the ice. She landed on her back and injured something. I know it required surgery, and her health insurance said it wouldn't pay, that she needed to make a claim on Jane and Rick's homeowner's policy. Well, Jane and Rick's insurance company insisted that Phoebe's own health insurance should cover it, and they all wound up in court. Jane and Rick knew it was just business, nothing personal, but it came at the time when Jane was just opening her shop, and it delayed a business loan she needed. There were allegations of neglect on Rick's part for not shoveling the walk better, and on Phoebe's part for being drunk that night, so by the time all the bills were paid there were a lot of hurt feelings. It took a while for everyone to relax again and socialize without a lot of tension. Eventually Jane got her loan and opened her shop, but there might still be some residual anger."

"Do you really think Rick would wait all these years to seek revenge?"

"No, I don't. To my knowledge, he's never done anything spiteful like that."

"Liz and Sylvia hate her, don't they?"

"Phoebe is slim, blonde, cute, and had just snagged an eligible bachelor, thinning out the available herd. What could they possible like about her?"

"Wow, that's mean."

"I'm being facetious. I like Phoebe, and most of the time, Sylvia and Liz like her too. Phoebe's divorce from Alastair was rough. She does like to drink though. If she'd leaned over the railing to be ill and fallen, Rick might not want to admit that he was too drunk to save her."

"Or didn't want to save her...But giving him the benefit of the doubt, wouldn't he have called for help?"

"Yes, I think he would have. So there goes that theory. I'm tired, let's talk more in the morning."

"Good idea. Maybe sleeping on all this will help."

It took me a few minutes of deep breathing to calm myself, and before long, I fell into a dreamless sleep.

CRUISE DAY FOUR

WEDNESDAY

CHAPTER EIGHT

Deck Thirteen

I awoke at three o'clock, unable to sleep any further. I was remembering that we hadn't gone back to the bars on deck thirteen to ask the waitresses if they'd seen Phoebe, although we now knew that she had been up there dancing with some strangers and with Rick. I was still perplexed at his keeping this information to himself when we first learned that Phoebe was missing.

Melinda was sleeping peacefully, so I decided to wander up to the bars myself. Even if they were closed now, the waitresses might still be cleaning up.

I got out of bed, dressed, combed my hair, and grabbed my ID card. I was able to leave without waking Melinda, wondering if this deceptive feeling was how Phoebe felt when she'd snuck out the other night.

The hallways were empty, as were the elevators to deck thirteen, but as I exited, I was amazed at the loud music still blaring from the disco bar and the crowds of young adults bumping and grinding with drinks in one hand and someone else's body part in another. The party was obviously far from over.

I shoved through the crowd to the bar and asked for a vodka and tonic.

"Too late," the bartender said. "Cola?"

"Okay."

I looked around in the semi-darkness as he squirted something dark into a clear plastic cup. Clutching the cup carefully to my chest, I wound my way back through the dancers and looked for a waitress. I noted that due to the semi-darkness and the density of the crowd, unless you were dancing within one or two feet of someone, you'd have no way of knowing who else was in the bar. The strobe, with its alternating bursts of light followed by immediate plunges into darkness, only added to the confusion.

On the fringes of the crowd, I found a young girl in spandex pants, black heels, pink halter top, and a tiny white apron tied around her waist mopping up the empty tables around the perimeter of the dance floor. I tapped her on the shoulder, and she spun around in surprise.

"Do you speak English?" I asked.

"Yes," she answered and smiled. "I'm from the Philippines."

"I was wondering if you remember seeing an older woman dancing here the other night. She was around fifty years old with pale blonde hair. She's very small...maybe dancing with some men?"

"I don't know," she said. "I see so many people. What was she wearing?"

"I don't know," I replied. "But this was the last place she was seen, and now she's missing."

"Oh, *that* lady. The one the captain is looking for. No, I didn't see her, but she could have been here."

"Thank you," I said and turned to leave.

That's when I saw her, through the glass, out on the balcony that skirted this section of the deck. I could barely make her out, but Phoebe was standing out there, wearing a slim, white, ankle-length dress. Her ash-blonde hair was feathered out from around her face like a halo. The edges of her thin mouth were turned down in sadness. It was the face I had seen in the porthole window while waiting to board. The hairs on my neck and arms stood up, and a ripple of fear swept over me.

I shouldered my way through all the dancers and went across the hallway to the glass door to the outside. When I got there, Phoebe was gone. I looked around me and didn't see her anywhere. In a panic, I looked left and right again, saw no one, and quickly ran to the side and looked over the railing, down to the promenade on deck twelve. No one was there.

I stood, tingling with confusion. I had seen Phoebe, seen her in a long white dress, its skirt swirling in the ocean breeze and her hair glowing in the moonlight. Where did she go?

Someone tapped me on the shoulder, and I jumped in surprise. I turned to see Sven standing behind me, his arm still raised.

"What are you doing here?" I gasped and then blurted out, "Did you see her? Did you see a woman in a white dress standing here?"

"No, I'm sorry, I only saw you...looking frantic. I didn't mean to startle you. Is anything wrong?"

"I thought I saw Phoebe, standing out here on the deck. But when I got here she was gone. I swear I didn't imagine it."

"What do you think happened to her?" he asked, putting his arm around my shoulder.

"I don't know." But I was left thinking that I had again seen an apparition, a request from Phoebe to me to keep searching.

Turning to Sven I said, "Everyone thinks she fell overboard."

"But, look..." he said, pointing. "She couldn't have fallen overboard from here. If she had gone over the railing she would have only landed on the promenade deck below. She wouldn't have gone into the water."

I looked again and saw that deck thirteen was of a smaller circumference than deck twelve. Anything going over the side would have had to be thrown eight or ten feet out over the promenade deck below to get to the water.

"Oh, you're right," I said, sighing with relief. I relaxed against him and suddenly felt Sven's lips brush my forehead. They were warm and soft, the perfect mix of gentleness and desire. Unfortunately, I was not in the mood for romance. I straightened up and gently pushed him back.

"I have to get back to my stateroom," I said.

"Can I walk you there?"

"No, thank you, but could you continue asking around about my friend?"

"Yes, and I'll even ask the captain tomorrow. Perhaps he'll tell me something that he didn't share with you. Captains can be quite jealous of their knowledge."

"I'd appreciate that. I'll talk to you tomorrow."

I returned to my stateroom, brain ablaze with the thought that she couldn't have fallen from deck thirteen without landing on deck twelve.

Knowing that Phoebe couldn't have fallen overboard from deck thirteen ruled out the video at 12:35 a.m. and narrowed down the possibilities. I wanted to wake up Melinda and tell her all this, but I didn't. Instead, I went to bed and thought about Sven's lips on my forehead. The cruise director! I was willing to bet he had already notched his bedpost down to nothing.

CHAPTER NINE
No More Clues

I woke up for the second time at eight o'clock. Melinda's bed was empty, so I assumed she had gone to breakfast. As I showered and dressed, I thought more about Phoebe and what motive anyone could possibly have to kill her. Or was it, perhaps, an accident after all, and no one had seen it?

As I waited for the elevator, another thought occurred to me. If it had been an accident, why was she appearing to me? My experiences in the past were that spirits showed themselves only when they had unfinished business. I'd heard Darcie Malone's father singing for her to come home long after both he and Darcie had died. I'd seen my friend Rosie's ghost when she wanted the person who caused her death to be punished. Phoebe's appearing to me seemed to suggest foul play, and her appearing in the porthole *before* she disappeared was doubly disturbing. I didn't want to think I'd been warned and could have acted to prevent whatever befell her.

When I arrived at the dining room, I saw Melinda, Sylvia, and Liz seated in a circle having breakfast. Melinda looked like she was still ill. Sylvia and Liz were complaining about their pancakes and syrup being cold. I waved to them, got myself a tray, and walked the buffet line, choosing coffee, cereal, and juice. Sitting down at the table I smiled at them and asked, "Jane and Rick still sleeping?"

"They're both sick," Melinda said. "Probably the Norovirus. Did everyone get a squirt of hand sanitizer before getting their breakfast?

We all murmured, "Yes, of course."

Sylvia suddenly jumped up. "I can't remember if I did or not. My hands feel all germy and weird. I'm going to get some more. I'll be right back."

"Can't be too careful," Liz murmured. "I think I'll get some more too." She immediately rose from the table and followed Sylvia to where the attendant stood by the door, squirting everyone's palms with the hygienic gel.

"Let's hope no one else comes down with it," I said, looking around at all the people enjoying breakfast. "I'm guessing it's not a ship-wide epidemic yet."

"I might stop eating altogether now," Melinda said, pushing her barely touched pancakes to the farside of her tray. "If I drink lots of liquids, maybe I can avoid it."

I didn't want to talk about the Norovirus that morning. "I have news," I announced.

"They found Phoebe?" Liz squeaked with surprise as she and Sylvia reseated themselves.

"No," I said, pouring milk on my cereal and taking a sip of juice. "But I went up to deck thirteen last night and looked over the railing. You can't fall from that deck into the ocean. The promenade on deck twelve juts out ten feet from underneath deck thirteen. Anything or anyone falling from thirteen would have landed on the walkway of deck twelve."

Melinda's eyebrows shot up. "Why didn't the captain tell us that?"

"Who knows?" I said. "Maybe he's too busy to attend to details. I think, though, that we can cross off the idea that something happened on deck thirteen."

"What were the other decks the captain described things falling from?" Liz asked, digging into a grapefruit.

"Deck eight and from the promenade on deck twelve," Melinda said. "But the deck eight video was from the first night we were here, not the night Phoebe disappeared. The deck twelve video was taken about the time Phoebe was last seen." She sipped her tea. "What do you all think?"

"I'm guessing a lover's quarrel," Liz shrugged, now starting on a dish of fresh fruit. "Maybe Duncan and Phoebe had another fight about Alastair, and Duncan snapped. He pushed her overboard and the exertion of doing that and his own guilt are what's causing his symptoms." She neatly shepherded three blueberries onto her spoon and dropped them in her mouth.

"That's awful," Melinda said. "How could you think such a thing?"

Liz didn't answer.

"No, I don't think that's what happened," Melinda continued. "I would be able to tell if Duncan were feeling those emotions, and I'm not feeling guilt. I'm feeling only shame and distress that such a thing would happen to him and that he's been unable to help."

"You've been wrong before," Sylvia said softly and followed her comment by stuffing the last of her pancakes into her mouth.

"Well, what do you think we should do today?" I asked to steer the conversation away from Melinda.

"Talk to our liaison. What's her name...Carlotta?" Sylvia said.

"Miss Carlisle," Liz said. "I'll call her later and let you know what she says."

"Thanks, Liz," Melinda replied for us. "I think Emily and I should do some more snooping. I want to double-check those places we weren't able to cover before." She turned to me, "You said you couldn't get behind the stage in the auditorium in the back of the ship, right? Let's see if we can find the lights and look back there. Does anybody have any other ideas?"

"I'm worn out with all this anxiety," Sylvia said. "If the captain can't find her, I don't think we can. I'd like to take a day to sit by the pool and try to enjoy just a little bit of this cruise until we have more information."

"How about you, Liz?" Melinda asked.

"I think I'll join her. There's really nothing else we can do for now."

Their day settled, Sylvia and Liz gathered up purses and pill containers and left Melinda and me. I sipped my coffee in silence for a few seconds then softly asked Melinda, "When have you been wrong?"

"It was years ago. When Sylvia's husband first became sick. She came to me and asked me if he was going to die. I told her no, and six months later, he was gone. She acted as if it were almost my fault." Melinda held her tea cup clutched in both hands and looked away from our table, out through the glass walls and off into the sky.

The filtered sunlight caught the fine wrinkles at the corners of her eyes and lit them up like pale white rivulets etched into the olive skin of her face. I could see the slight purple bruising of sleeplessness cradled below her hazel eyes. There had not been much pleasure in this cruise for Melinda so far.

"She asked you to predict the future," I said. "My understanding of your gift is that you can't do that."

"No, I can't. But, when I was with her husband, he seemed to exude such confidence when he spoke about his treatments, and he was so certain that he was being cured, that I misinterpreted all that optimism as a positive result. I knew at the time that I shouldn't give Sylvia false assurances, but what do you say to a friend who is frantic with worry? If I were anyone else, she would have known that I was just being kind. Because of my so-called gift, she thought it was the truth. She's never totally forgiven me."

"I'm so sorry. You've managed to stay friends, though. Maybe time will heal her."

"Let's hope so."

"And are you getting any feelings now from anyone in our group that indicates guilt?"

"I'm not ready to say anything definite yet. I can't be wrong again." She took a sip of tea and smiled at me sadly over the rim of the cup.

"Okay, I understand." I put down my empty coffee mug. "Let's go look for Phoebe."

We made our way via elevators and hallways to the auditorium at the back of deck nine. Some kind of presentation was in progress: a small crowd of vacationers were seated in front of the orchestra pit watching a slide show about paintings. A brown-suited man stood at the podium. He held a pointer and seemed to be leading a discussion about the artwork on the screen. Melinda and I slipped down a side aisle and followed an exit sign that led to a hallway in one direction or led backstage if you went the opposite way. Melinda and I quietly made our way backstage.

Because of the seminar, the back stage was partially illuminated. The dim lighting revealed a mishmash of scenery, chairs, tables, ladders, and stand-alone lamps. Melinda and I tiptoed around each item and found a back wall painted black and covered with switches and dials. As we explored, we found rope pulleys for the curtains and a scattering of fake plants and ferns. There was no body — not Phoebe's or anyone else's.

We gave up and left, deciding to check out the other auditorium at the front of the ship. It was dark since it was not being used for our cruise, but having inspected its twin, we were now able to find our way to the stage, up the side steps, and to the back wall with the light switches. Melinda, slightly ahead of me, felt her way along the wall. I heard a click and suddenly whoosh — the back stage lit up.

"Hey!" A male voice cried out. We turned to find its source and there was Sven, on a plush gray sofa, with his naked posterior poised in the air. Recovering from that, I next noticed the pale limbs of an unknown woman beneath him. *Busted*, I thought and couldn't help smiling. Before I could comment, Melinda snapped the switch back to the off position.

"Let's get out of here," she muttered, but I could hear her giggling as we retraced our steps back out of the auditorium.

When we got outside the doors, we leaned against the walls and collapsed laughing.

"Did you ever?" Melanie gasped.

"No, that's a first," I replied, as we tried to regain our composure.

I kept waiting for Sven to appear and admonish us, but he never did. I guess he just resumed what he'd been doing. I wondered if he had recognized me. Well, it didn't matter. The picture of him on that couch is going to stay with me forever, and I doubt I'll ever think of his kiss on my forehead the same way again.

"Well, now what?" I finally asked.

"Let's ask Duncan if we can search his room again for clues. I know we've been in the bathroom and looked at their bureau drawers, but I'd like to examine everything again, including the balcony."

In the infirmary, the receptionist, recognizing us, waved us through, to the consternation of half a dozen folk waiting to be seen.

We entered Duncan's room and were appalled at what we found. Duncan, panicky eyes darting wildly around, was leaning forward over his meal tray with both arms to support himself, his face covered in sweat, his mouth wide open. His head and chest reared up as he gasped for air.

Melinda went to him, while I ran out of the room shouting for the doctor. She appeared instantly from another room and rushed past me. She carried a syringe, and as Melinda held Duncan's left hand, the doctor plunged the needle into his right arm.

It seemed to help a little as Duncan's chest slowed just a bit and the wild look left his eyes.

"I'll have to get the respiratory therapist back," the doctor said to us. "Please leave us alone. I'm doing my best to keep your friend alive until we reach St. Thomas in the morning."

"Oh no," I said to Melinda as we left the room. "He's worse than before. What will we do if he dies?"

"Let's not think about that," Melinda replied, showing me Duncan's ID card. "This was sitting out on his nightstand. Let's go."

We opened the door to Duncan and Phoebe's stateroom slowly and quietly, as if we were expecting one of them to be inside. Once in, we turned on all the lights and opened the drapes to their balcony. Glancing outside, the sun was a perfect orange disc of warmth and good will. If only our cruise could have been as splendid.

We decided to split the room between us and examine every square inch, starting from the doorway, all along the walls, and ending at the balcony railing. After searching through the couple's personal items and Phoebe's cosmetics, and getting down on my hands and knees to peer into every corner of the floor, I found nothing that I could call a clue.

My side of the room included the bureau drawers and one single bed, Melinda's side the desk and the other single bed. We pulled out clothes and felt in all the pockets, even tore the bedclothes off to shake them out — all to no avail. I slid my fingers in between the cushions of the small couch and felt along the floor.

Melinda inspected the top and bottom of the coffee table, throwing the now wilted flowers into a trash can she had already searched. She reopened the note that had come with the flowers and repeated its words softly:

Fair of skin is not pure of heart
Blue eyes see little in the dark
When blood turns black and eyes burn green
Beware the secrets now unseen.

"You know..." Melinda said when she'd finished reading the poem again, "it's as if the writer is accusing either Phoebe or Duncan of something. I wonder what it is."

"We might know that," I replied, "if we knew who wrote the note. The writer also talks about green eyes, which is a symbol of jealousy. But I don't know what black blood means."

"In a general sense, blood means life and black means death, so my guess is something alive turns into something dead."

"That sounds spooky...a foretelling of Phoebe...someone alive, turning black into someone dead. The writer of that note seems to know that Phoebe is going to die."

"Or Duncan," Melinda said as she opened the sliding glass door.

"Well, we still have the balcony to examine."

There wasn't much to examine, just two white plastic chairs and a matching table. We checked the corners, along the railing, and over the side. Below us the dark Atlantic rushed by, deeper than the Rockies were tall and colder than any place on earth except the poles. It too held mysteries we might never learn. Did it hide Phoebe and her secrets as well?

"Nothing," I observed.

"Hmmm...Well, let's get some lunch," Melinda suggested.

"Aye, aye, cap."

As we walked the hallway to the elevator, Melinda suddenly said, "I have an idea."

"What?"

"Let's hold a séance tonight in Duncan and Phoebe's room. The six of us together might be able to get through to the other side. Maybe someone will talk to us and tell us what happened."

"Might help," I said. "Let's see if they're at lunch."

When we got to deck twelve, we looked for a table after getting our lunch. We saw Jane and Rick seated at a table for two, deep in conversation. Neither Sylvia nor Liz was in sight.

We walked up to them with our trays and Melinda greeted them with, "Hey, Jane! Hey, Rick! How are you two doing? Feeling better?"

Jane put down her tea and shook her head. I noticed both she and Rick had only saltines and tea for lunch. I supposed that was all they could manage. But should they have been out of their stateroom if they did have the Norovirus? I thought it better not to ask as we might be overheard and cause a panic.

"We saw Liz and she talked with Ms. Carlisle," Jane said, ignoring Melinda's questions. "There's no news. She only said that we'll be in St. Thomas by seven o'clock tomorrow morning, and the ship will be met by members of the US Coast Guard, a representative of the territorial governor, and an ambulance for Duncan. His family has been contacted and his son, Justin, will be waiting at the hospital for his father."

"Will the Coast Guard search the ship?" Melinda asked.

"She wouldn't say, but she did request that we be discreet and not talk about Phoebe's disappearance to the crew or passengers. She's afraid some passengers may choose to leave the cruise since they can make other arrangements once we're in port. I told her that, of course, we wouldn't say anything."

"I can't promise that," Melinda said.

"Suit yourself," Rick said with an attitude of dismissal. He lifted his cup and sipped his tea.

"I have a suggestion that I want to run by everyone at dinner tonight. Will you be there?" Melinda asked.

"Of course," Jane said.

"Okay, see you then," Melinda replied, and we headed for a table of our own.

"Well, they seem well enough to be out of their stateroom. I guess they're not too sick."

"No, and I'm glad. If they had the Norovirus, they'd be much sicker, so I guess it's not that."

"Not very concerned about Phoebe or Duncan, are they?" I noted.

"No, they're not. That bothers me too."

"They could still be arguing about Rick's going dancing the other night."

"Hopefully it won't cause too much damage to their relationship." Melinda sighed.

We couldn't find Liz or Sylvia, so we sat at a table for two and tried to enjoy our chicken sandwiches and strawberry salads.

"I think we should take this afternoon off," Melinda said, as she stretched and polished off the last berry. I was glad to see that her appetite was back.

"We need to relax and perhaps that'll prompt some creative thinking. I also want to consider how to conduct this séance tonight."

"May I suggest we put on bathing suits and sit by the pool? Maybe with a cool drink?"

"Yes, let's."

After lunch we returned to our stateroom to change and made the trip back to deck twelve. Once settled in the last two empty lounge chairs next to each other, we flagged down a waiter. I ordered a margarita and a glass of water. Melinda got a beer and a coke. Reggae music blared from the loudspeakers where invisible hands patted bongos and vibes clinked musically in the background. A perfect cruise...if only...

CHAPTER TEN
A Clue at Last!

I woke up with a start to cold water trickling onto my face. Sven stood above me in plaid bathing trunks with a tray in one hand and a dripping glass of pink something in the other.

"Another drink, milady?" he asked.

"Thank you," I said as I sat up. He handed the pink drink to me and sat down on the lower half of the lounge chair. My head was reeling with the embarrassing question of whether he had recognized me earlier. I was guessing not, as he smiled and took a second pink drink and a cola from the tray and deposited them on the table that Melinda and I were sharing. Melinda continued to sleep.

Sven placed the tray underneath the lounge chair and, picking up the cola, asked, "Did you find your lady friend?"

"No. Did you hear anything?"

"Well, I've asked around and can tell you a few things. She was first seen dancing on deck thirteen with a group of Slavic gentlemen. Then another man...in your party...saw her and started dancing with her. Then he left, and she was seen later arguing with two women. My informant said one was thin and one was...ah... not thin."

Liz and Sylvia I guessed.

"Did anyone hear what they were arguing about?"

"No, they couldn't make out what the problem was. But I did find something, if you want to take a look at it. After hearing about the argument, I took a walk around decks twelve and thirteen to examine the railings. At several spots along the promenade there are life preservers attached to the railings for use in an emergency."

"Is one of them missing?"

"No, but on deck twelve one had a few strands of light blond hair entwined in the rope that attaches it to the railing. Would you like to see it?"

"Yes!" I stood up immediately and put down my drink. Sven kept his as we threaded our way through the sunbathers and running children. Following the promenade around the outside of the day care and the gym, we came to a more secluded place where one would be partially out of the sight of those by the pool. Sven stopped at a life preserver maybe three feet in diameter with *Galleon of the Galaxy* emblazoned on it in blue letters. I looked up to deck thirteen above us and saw that we were directly underneath the disco bar.

Sven pointed to the ropes securing the life preserver to the railing, and sure enough, there were three or four long blonde hairs entwined there.

"Sven, this is great! The hairs look exactly like Phoebe's. Should I keep them, or will you?"

"I'll take them. I just wanted you to see them first." With that, Sven took a small clear plastic bag from his pocket and carefully removed the hairs. After putting the hairs in the bag, he returned it to his pocket.

"Could we speak to the person who told you about the argument they witnessed?"

"I'm afraid not. She won't come forward. She hasn't spoken to the captain either, and I promised her I wouldn't reveal her name. She's part of the staff, and she's afraid of being dismissed if there should be a scandal involving any of the passengers."

I briefly wondered if it was the woman he had been with earlier in the morning.

"Okay, I understand that. But I have one more question. Were the Slavic gentlemen Phoebe was dancing with ever identified? Maybe they had something to do with her disappearance; they could have even kidnapped her."

"Yes, they have been identified. They're engineers on holiday. They were questioned and their cabins searched. We found nothing. And no one has come forward to say they were seen with your friend at any other time that night, or after."

"Well, okay. Thank you."

"Will you have a drink with me later tonight after the show, around ten thirty?" he asked. "I'll meet you in the disco bar on deck thirteen."

What could I say? This man (with the fetching derrière) had just done me a tremendous favor. "Of course, I'd be glad to."

"See you then," he said and walked off.

"Melinda," I called softly as I shook her awake. "I can't wait to tell you what's been found."

After I related what Sven had shown me, Melinda said, "I've had a thought you might not like."

"That's okay. What is it?"

"I don't have good feelings about Sven. His aura is a muddy pink. That tells me he's dishonest and immature. Do you think he might have planted these hairs? Could he be responsible for Phoebe's disappearance or covering up for a crew member who harmed her?"

"Oh my, you're right. We can't trust him. Maybe he's misleading us on purpose. What would his motive be, though?"

"Maybe he made a pass at her and she rejected him."

"He's quite the Romeo, but we don't know for sure that those hairs even belong to Phoebe. They could just look like hers."

"True. Without a DNA analysis, we can't prove that they're Phoebe's," Melinda said. "There's certainly lots of blonds on this cruise. We're going to need more than just this for proof that he or anyone did something to Phoebe."

"You know the group better than I. Can you think of any reason one of them would want to harm Phoebe? What do you suppose Phoebe, Liz, and Sylvia were arguing about?"

"I have no idea."

"Should we just confront Sylvia and Liz?"

"I'm not sure 'confront' is the best idea. Maybe we should just have a talk." She looked at her watch. "It's about time to start getting dressed for dinner. Why don't we stop at their stateroom 'on our way' to ours?"

It was a trek to the other end of the ship to Sylvia and Liz's cabin 8103. Luckily, they were both there and shouted "Come in" when we knocked. We found them sitting on their balcony with their feet up on the railing, each holding a martini.

"The cruise director, whom Emily has made a friend of," Melinda said, winking at me, "found something of interest on deck twelve. It looks like some of Phoebe's hair. It was stuck in the rope of a life preserver that's mounted on the railing. He also said someone saw two women arguing with Phoebe on deck twelve the night she disappeared. Could it have been you two?"

"No, not us," they said in unison, like Tweedle Dum and Tweedle Dee.

"Are you sure?" I asked, pointedly. Both shook their heads and remained silent, a clear indication that they had nothing more to say and that our presence was not welcome. After waiting four or five seconds in uncomfortable silence, Melinda and I left. I have to admit that I was perplexed by their lack of interest.

Back in the hallway, making the long trek to our stateroom, Melinda observed, "They seemed so perfectly in tune with each other, I feel as if they do know something and have agreed to keep quiet about it."

"Well, I guess they don't care much for Phoebe if they don't even want to find out what happened to her."

"Unless, of course, they do know what happened to her and it implicates them."

"We'll have to think of a way to get them to crack."

"I'm hoping the séance will do just that."

Dinner was a silent affair. The good news was that it was lobster night, and guests were allowed to order seconds and even thirds if they wanted. As I only like the tail portion, I ordered two. Jane and Rick asked for bullion and crackers only.

I hazarded a question. "Still fighting that virus?"

"Oh, we're not sick," Jane said. "We've started a new diet. Both Rick and I feel that we could lose a few pounds."

"Good luck," Liz teased. "I think I've managed to maintain my pre-cruise weight."

"Well, I certainly need to lose a few, cruise or no," Jane acknowledged.

"And I'm not going to let her diet alone," Rick added.

As the last dinner plate was cleared away, Dmitri told us that for lobster night, dessert was always Baked Alaska served up with a parade and music. As he spoke, the lights went out. The crowd hushed as we were enveloped in sudden darkness. All at once, twenty waiters appeared, pushing twenty wheeled carts in a circle around the dining room. Each cart carried a Baked Alaska with the white meringue set afire, the small flames dancing and swaying as they moved, reflecting red and orange against the stark whiteness of the waiters' jackets. To add to the excitement, piped-in music pounded out the 1812 Overture as the waiters ran the circumference of the floor. At the climax, where the music soars and the canons roar, a tray was delivered to each table, flames blazing in the chill, refrigerated air. Seconds later, the flames died out and the lights came back on. All the diners broke into spontaneous applause.

The dramatic presentation made our cake that much more delicious as Dmitri did the honors and sliced a piece for each of us, and seconds as well if we wanted them. I felt sorry for Jane and Rick who chose not to partake. They ordered only black coffee for dessert.

As we dawdled over the devil's food cake and ice cream, Liz looked up from hers and said to Jane, "Didn't see much of you and Rick today. Catching up on your reading?"

Jane blushed. "Well, to tell you the truth, not really." She glanced at Rick as if looking for approval for what she was about to say. "We sort of stayed in bed all afternoon."

"Why not?" I commented. "This is vacation."

"We weren't just napping," Rick said.

"Of course not," Liz said with a smile. "We know what you were doing."

"Not exactly," Jane continued. "You know I was a little angry at Rick for going dancing with Phoebe...and for a few other things." She looked at Rick and he shrugged.

"Guilty as charged," he said, between sips of coffee.

"Well, I wanted to iron out some issues before they turned into more difficult problems...you know the kind...which fester over time and come back to haunt you. We all say 'it's okay' or 'I'll get over it,' but often we don't."

I certainly knew what she was talking about; I imagine we all did.

"Well, do you remember when that movie star Fanny Malloy and her husband almost split over his infidelity? I saw her on TV soon after that, and she said they settled their problems by going to bed and agreeing to *stay* in bed until the issue was resolved. And it worked! They're still together."

"Great idea!" Melinda interrupted.

"Yes," Jane continued. "So that's what Rick and I did, and it worked for us too." She gave us a beaming grin. Rick looked a trifle embarrassed.

"Congratulations!" I said, raising my hands and clapping. "It's so good to hear that you two have the faith in each other to tackle the hard problems and commit to their resolution. It's too bad more couples can't do that."

"Yes," Melinda agreed and raised her own hands in soft applause.

"Sounds like some bull to me," Liz commented. "But if it works for you, go for it."

Leave it to Liz to spoil a good vibe.

Melinda chose this moment to announce her plan for a séance that night in Phoebe and Duncan's room.

"No way!" was Liz's response.

"I'm not into that," said Sylvia.

"Do you even know how to do one?" Rick asked.

"Yes. I had a friend who was a Wiccan, and she showed me how to conduct one."

"Don't we need a medium?" Jane inquired.

"No, actually we don't. They don't have to be like the ones in movies. We'll sit together and hold hands, but there won't be voices speaking out of thin air or objects moving around. I won't lose consciousness and be taken over by another spirit. What we'll do is just sit quietly. You want to try and clear your mind and be receptive to whatever thoughts pop into your head. If a spirit is trying to contact us, he or she will plant thoughts in our minds. Then, after twenty minutes or so, we'll break the circle and discuss what thoughts we had. There's nothing scary about it at all."

"So," Rick said, "How do we know what information is spirit-driven and what's just that person's private thoughts?"

"We'll know we've got something if we all wind up thinking the same thing."

"We already know Phoebe's missing," Jane spoke up. "So we're all going to be thinking about that anyway."

"It's hard to tell you what's going to happen." Melinda sighed and, still sensing reluctance, added, "I'm asking for just twenty minutes of your time to sit quietly in a circle. I'd like to, at least, give it a chance. We don't have any other leads."

"Well, if I refuse I'll look like I've got something to hide," Liz said. "I'm in."

"Me too." This was from Sylvia.

Jane and Rick looked at each with questioning eyes. "I guess we're in too," Rick said.

"Okay," Melinda continued. "I'll meet you at Phoebe and Duncan's room at nine o'clock."

CHAPTER ELEVEN

SEANCE

By nine o'clock that evening, the sun had descended into the arms of the cotton-soft clouds on the western horizon. I gazed at the sunset wistfully as I viewed the few remaining violet puffs of cumulus from Phoebe and Duncan's balcony doors. I wished I felt as peaceful as the sunset looked. I stood there and left the drapes open only long enough for us all to find a seat on the beds, then I shut them tightly. The room was in total darkness. Everyone was silent.

I knew Melinda was perched on the coffee table that had been moved in between the two beds, so I found my way to the small empty chair that belonged to the desk. Jane and Rick were sitting on one single bed, and Liz and Sylvia on the other, facing Jane and Rick. In this way we formed a clumsy circle. At Melinda's word, we reached out and joined hands. I was surprised Melinda hadn't included a candle, but maybe I was thinking of a movie version of a séance.

Melinda began, "We send out our love to Phoebe, to her family, and to all who are acquainted with her—those living and those who have passed over. It is our love for Phoebe that brings us here tonight. Our love for Phoebe that prompts us to ask where she is. Phoebe...if you can...acknowledge our love, and let us know how we can find you. Thank you."

We stayed in silence, the quiet broken only occasionally by the creak of the ship's hull or a voice in the hall. As the silence continued and deepened, I felt Rick's left hand, which clutched my right one, grow tense and then relax. To my other side was Liz, whose hand was rigid. I felt she was trying to block any information that might come through. I wondered if her negative energy would doom our chances to learn something new.

The silence seemed to fill with emotion, I could sense fear mingled with panic. I saw in my mind's eye a sparkling object fall from a railing of the ship. Then I saw Phoebe standing below it. A shadow appeared. I heard her gasp in surprise. Her surprise turned to dismay as the shadow overtook her. Then I sensed nothing more.

After thirty seconds of no stimuli, I suddenly heard a baby crying. Was it in the hallway? Was it next door? Was it real or only a figment of my imagination? It wailed softly for just a moment or two, then stopped, and all was quiet again.

Someone in our group inhaled sharply, then I heard a whispered "No." I thought it might have come from Jane.

Melinda spoke up, "We are not all in accord. Some of us are afraid. Please trust in the love we have for one another. Open your hearts. Let Phoebe come through."

Suddenly Rick burst out, "This is nonsense. I'm leaving."

Still groggy with our thoughts, no one spoke as we heard him get up and fumble for the door.

"Blasted door," he cursed, as he struggled with the handle.

"I'm with the baby," came a voice from nowhere, floating in the air above our heads. It sounded like Phoebe. Liz let go of my hand and screamed.

"No, you're not!" Rick shouted. Finally, he was able to wrench the door open, and he fled down the hall. We heard his heavy footsteps sprinting on the carpet as if distance was his only salvation. *You can run,* I thought, in the words of the old cliché, *but you can't hide.*

Light from the hallway flooded into the room, and we sat in shock, the circle broken, our ears echoing with the voice Melinda said we wouldn't hear. Phoebe had spoken. She was with the baby. What baby?

Melinda got up and turned on the desk light. She went to the door and closed it.

"Please, don't anyone move just yet," she said. "I want you to tell me what was in the minds of each of you while the lights were out."

Jane was the first to speak. "It's too personal. I can't share. And it didn't have anything to do with Phoebe's disappearance."

"I heard a baby crying," said Sylvia. "Did anyone else?"

"I did," I said. "I saw something shiny fall from the ship. Then I saw Phoebe. There was also a black shadow that seemed to swallow her up. I could feel her surprise, then her terror."

"That's crazy," Liz said. "It was just your imagination creating an explanation for what's happened."

"Yes, it could be," I admitted. "But why would I imagine a baby crying?"

"It's all nonsense," Jane said and stood up. "I'm going to find Rick. This hasn't helped at all. It's only made matters worse." She left, her words ringing in my head.

"What about you, Melinda?" I asked. "What were your thoughts?"

"I heard the baby crying too, but I also felt things. Sylvia, you have probably known Phoebe longer than any of us. Did she lose a baby?"

"She had an abortion." Sylvia spoke softly and sadly, perhaps the only time I'd heard her speak of Phoebe without rancor. "When we were in high school. No one else knows. Even her parents didn't know."

"And the father was?" I asked.

"I promised not to tell, but I think someone's behavior here tonight made it pretty clear."

"Does Jane know?"

"If she didn't, she does now."

Rick. Rick had fathered a baby with Phoebe, and she'd had an abortion. This was terrible news, but I couldn't see it being a motive for murder.

"Jane and Rick never had children, did they?" I asked.

"No," Liz said. "Jane's womb was damaged by endometriosis."

"Would Rick be afraid for some reason that Phoebe would tell Jane? Although this doesn't seem like the time or place for that."

"I agree," said Melinda. "Phoebe was on her honeymoon. Why would anyone bring up something that had happened in high school with another man? On the other hand, would Rick have threatened to tell Duncan, and Phoebe didn't want him to? I think Duncan is Catholic. He might not approve of abortion. Could Duncan and Phoebe have quarreled about that?"

"But, again..." I asked, "why now? It doesn't make sense."

"If Phoebe is dead," Melinda continued, "And there was a baby, it would be understandable that now she has been reunited with her baby on the other side."

I didn't know how to respond to that, and no one else spoke either, probably for the same reason. I was open to the possibility of souls reuniting after death, but it wasn't a firm belief. I was also still hoping that Phoebe would be found alive.

We sat for a few more moments in silence.

"If no one else has anything to say, then I guess that's it," Melinda said.

Liz sighed, "I'm tired and going to bed."

"I'm coming with you," Sylvia addressed Liz. Then, to us, "Good night, all."

"I'm tired, too" I said to Melinda. "But I promised Sven I'd meet him for a drink in the disco bar. Care to join us?"

"No, but be careful." She smiled, probably remembering what we'd seen this morning. "He might be a suspect. I actually have another date with Elvis."

"Have fun."

"I will," she replied and started out into the hallway. I soon remembered that in our haste to have the séance, we'd forgotten about Duncan. I went down to deck two, but the doors to the infirmary were closed and locked. I considered calling the number posted on the door to use if there were an emergency. Since it wasn't, I headed back to the elevators.

On deck seven, the lady from the German band got on, holding a trombone. I smiled at her.

"Performing tonight?" I asked.

"Not in the auditorium. We're setting up on deck twelve for the midnight buffet. You should join us."

"Maybe I will, if I can stay awake."

"Have you found your friend yet?"

"No, and we've about given up hope. All I can figure is that somehow she fell overboard."

"It happens," she sighed. "Last year I read about two separate instances of passengers going overboard, but I don't think it was this cruise line. I believe their bodies were never found."

The elevator door opened for deck twelve and she exited. I had to admit it certainly seemed like Phoebe had met a similar fate.

When I got to the disco bar, it was only ten o'clock, but Sven was already there, sitting by himself at the bar, talking to the woman dispensing drinks. I sat down on the stool next to his.

"Too early?" I asked.

"Never," he said. "What would you like to drink?"

"Vodka and tonic, please."

The bartender was within earshot, and she turned to acknowledge my order.

"How is your search going?" Sven asked.

"We just held a séance in Phoebe's room. The results were not much help. Has anyone ever gone missing on this ship before?"

"A few years ago," he began, choosing not to comment on the séance. "A young woman left her boyfriend for another man she met on board. She hid out in his stateroom for three days. We did find her eventually, but the captain was quite upset. We're not allowed to speak of it. He wants his ship's reputation to be spotless."

The bartender placed the drink in front of me. Then Sven nudged me and pointed toward the outside deck. Melinda sat across from Elvis at a small table. They appeared to be chatting happily. The moonlight caught his hair and turned it into a cap of glowing white light sitting atop his high cheekbones and long face. He looked quite regal.

They were sitting not far from where I had seen Phoebe the other night. Had it really been her or merely someone with light hair? Perhaps the moonlight had played a trick on me.

I turned my attention back to Sven. "Is that any good?" I asked him, pointing at the "Non-Alcoholic" label on the bottle.

"Not really, but staff aren't allowed to drink alcohol while on the ship."

"I didn't know that. Must be tough."

"You get used to it."

"I want to ask you about Captain Bonaparte. When we arrive in St. Thomas tomorrow morning, he'll have to report what's happened to Phoebe. I'm very disappointed that he hasn't been more involved. After we were referred to Miss Carlisle, it's as if Phoebe's disappearance never happened. She doesn't call with any updates about what they're doing to find her."

"Does your friend have next of kin on board?"

"Her husband, Duncan, but he's in the infirmary with breathing problems."

"It's possible that the captain's not comfortable giving information to anyone except the next of kin, and since the husband is in the infirmary, he might think that he's too ill to handle it."

"Oh geez, I hate to think we're going to go home with no more information."

"See that guy over there with black hair, talking to the bartender?

That's Chester. He's in the Video Security department. Let's talk to him."

We moved down two bar stools to say hello to a young man with dark good looks. He had the disheveled mien of a techie. His hair was a trifle too long and hadn't seen a comb recently. His solid black sport shirt was wrinkled and partially unbuttoned. He wore torn blue jeans with black and white Chuck Taylors. Sven introduced me and added, "She's with the party that reported a woman missing yesterday. I know the captain had you pull surveillance video for that night. I recall you saw a few interesting things."

"Do you want to see the footage?" he asked.

"Yes, please, that would be wonderful," I replied.

"Let's go," he said and picked up his own bottle of half-empty N.A. beer.

Sven and I grabbed our drinks and followed Chester out to the elevators where we found one marked "Staff Only." We took this down to deck three where much of the ship's inner workings appeared to be housed. The Video Security room was dark and empty. Chester flicked on the lights, and we followed him to a tiny cubicle where he started up his computer.

"You know we not supposed to be here," he admonished me. "I'm doing this as a favor to Sven."

"My lips are sealed."

He clicked on a folder labeled 07JUN, which contained three files: Deck Four: 0001, Deck Thirteen: 0040, and Deck Twelve: 0045. He clicked on Deck Four first, which had the footage gathered from the security camera on the promenade. In deepening mist, you could see a heavyset young man leaning over the railing and being repeatedly ill.

"It's clearly not your missing friend," Chester said. "Let's look at deck thirteen next."

The picture was cloudy, but we could discern two or three blurred figures talking together. Suddenly one of them dropped something shiny and the others reacted. The object could have been keys, silverware, or jewelry. We couldn't see what happened to it, but suddenly everyone was looking over the railing of deck thirteen to the deck below. Then we saw the figures going down the steps that connect deck thirteen to deck twelve.

"What do you think it was that fell?" I asked.

"A piece of silverware is my guess," Chester replied. "We

lose hundreds of pieces of silverware on each trip. Now the most interesting footage...deck twelve."

"What time is it here?" I asked.

"Around 12:45 a.m., just minutes later. Now, this footage is also hampered by the fact that the group is partially obscured by the steps that connect deck twelve to deck thirteen. This is directly below where the people in the previous footage were standing on deck thirteen. Look carefully and you'll see three people walk past the camera and then become obscured by the steps. There's no way to identify them. I can't even make out if they're male or female.

"Now they look like they're squatting or kneeling on the ground, like they're searching for something. This goes on for a few minutes. Then they get up, and two people separate and leave the area. Then another figure appears...someone returning or a new person...joining the one left behind. Unfortunately, our resolution is not good enough to distinguish faces, and these old computers don't have a zoom function.

"Next, you see figures moving close together, and something goes over the railing. However, I have to stress that it could be anything...a sweater, a jacket, or even a towel. A figure, or maybe two figures, move on, and no one comes back into view."

"It looks to me as if two figures were definitely there, and then all of a sudden, there was one," I said. "That movement could have been Phoebe being pushed overboard."

"Or, again, someone being ill," Chester said. "I can't tell you how many times a day that happens on cruises. The footage just isn't clear enough to assume there were two people and that someone was lifted over the railing."

"If we *are* seeing a person go overboard, could she have jumped?" Sven asked. "That happens too."

"I don't think so," I replied. "Phoebe was on her honeymoon. None of her friends have mentioned any problems between her and her husband. I wish the captain had made these tapes available to us."

"As I said," Sven repeated, "there's nothing definite here, and we have no witnesses coming forward to corroborate this. You certainly couldn't prove anything in a court of law."

"Thank you both so much," I said to the men. "I have to tell Melinda about this."

"But you didn't get this information from me," Chester reminded me.

"No, I'll make something up. Don't worry. Thank you again," and, nodding to both, I left.

When I got to our stateroom, Melinda was back, comfortably sitting in bed and reading a book.

"How was your date with Elvis? Love that name."

"Wonderful. We have a lot in common...at least, superficially. We like the same music, read the same books, have seen the same movies. I really enjoyed myself. I'm feeling much better."

"I'm so glad! Maybe he'll visit you in New Hampshire. It's only six hours...not too bad a drive for a three- or four-day weekend."

I told her about the surveillance footage and instructed that she couldn't tell anyone how I learned about it.

"Shall we assume it was Phoebe going overboard on deck twelve?" I asked.

"Yes, I've felt from the beginning that she was dead. But I had no proof. However, even if that tape does show Phoebe being pushed overboard, we still don't know who could have done it."

"Could one of your friends be capable of this?"

"I don't know. I've been thinking about it. I can't rule out anyone...friend or stranger." Melinda sighed and then suddenly gulped, "Oh, don't forget that Duncan is going to the hospital in the morning."

"That's right. Oh my." I stifled a yawn. "I'm beat. I can't think about it anymore. Maybe we'll have more ideas in the morning."

CRUISE DAY FIVE

THURSDAY

CHAPTER TWELVE

CHARLOTTE AMALIE

The phone woke us both up at four thirty. Melinda went to the desk and answered it, spoke softly, and then hung up. She turned to see me sitting up in bed.

"That was Miss Carlisle. We've docked in St. Thomas. An ambulance is waiting to take Duncan to the hospital. She thinks someone should go with him. I told her we would go. Is that okay?"

"Of course."

"We'll only stay until Duncan's son, Justin, arrives. Then we'll come back to the ship."

"Okay."

We dressed quickly and went down to the infirmary. From the hallway, we could see an open cargo door onto the dock, and through that, we could see Duncan's stretcher being loaded into an ambulance. We stopped where a woman from Security was waiting to scan our badges before we left the ship. Someone, probably Miss Carlisle, had also ordered a taxi for Melinda and me. I was surprised that a representative of the ship wasn't coming with us, but I guess that wasn't procedure.

We connected with Duncan in the hospital's ER where he was in a bed in a makeshift room created by a white curtain on a semicircular track. He was hooked up to an IV, oxygen, and a blood pressure monitor. He gave us a big smile when he saw us. I guess he thought he might be on his own.

Right away he asked about Phoebe. We had to tell him that we still hadn't found her.

"I think something awful has happened to her," he said. "But I can't imagine what or why. I'm preparing myself for the worst."

We nodded at him in sad agreement, but didn't update him on our search. We didn't want to upset him any further.

Melinda and I had wisely brought books, so while Duncan rested we sat and read. Doctors and nurses wandered in every twenty minutes or so to check his vitals and told us they were glad to see that Duncan was breathing well.

Leaving so early, Melinda and I had not eaten breakfast, so at noontime, when an aide appeared with a tray for Duncan and proceeded to assist him with eating, we went looking for the hospital cafeteria. We never found it, but we did find a gift shop with a tearoom. The choices were few, but we managed to find prewrapped ham sandwiches, cartons of juice, and potato chips.

"I wonder when Justin is going to get here," I asked.

"Who knows? I thought he was going to be waiting for us."

When we finished, we returned to Duncan's curtained cubicle. He looked glum.

"You just missed the ship's agent, Miss Carlisle," he said. "Justin's plane has been delayed in San Juan. He won't be here until tomorrow. You can go back to the ship. I'll be okay. She left me a change of clothes. The rest of my and Phoebe's things will be packed up and sent back to the States."

Melinda and I looked at each other. "You should go back to the ship," she said to me. "Or take a walk through Charlotte Amalie. You might enjoy it. I can stay with Duncan."

"Not by myself. Besides, I'd be too worried. I'll stay here for now."

When the next doctor came by, I asked when Duncan would be moved to a hospital room.

"There's nothing available until later today," he answered while busy scribbling on Duncan's chart.

Melinda and I spent the next few hours reading, talking with Duncan, and fighting boredom. When Duncan slept, we discussed going back to the ship. However, neither of us felt comfortable leaving him in a US hospital that still managed to feel foreign.

Around four in the afternoon, two orderlies arrived with the news that a room had opened up for Duncan. We followed them as they steered Duncan's bed through the hallways, onto an elevator, and up to the fourth floor. Duncan's new address was a sunny yellow room with a large window and a view of the sea. It was also, thankfully, a private room, and a nurse was waiting for him so she could reattach the IV, oxygen, and blood pressure monitor.

"You don't have to stay any longer," she said to us. "I'll be checking on Mr. Blumen tonight. You can come back in the morning."

She looked reliably professional in her neat white uniform, so we took her advice and left after giving Duncan quick hugs. We caught a taxi and headed back to the ship.

"Thank God that's over," I said. "Now we can relax."

"What about Phoebe?" Melinda reminded me.

"You're right. No relaxing. But I am looking forward to dinner."

The dining room was almost empty when we arrived at our table. As we ordered drinks followed by dinner, no one else appeared. We didn't even have our regular waiter, Dmitri. A pretty young woman with a Scandinavian accent explained that Dimitri had been given shore leave for the evening.

There was no show that night. Even the casinos were closed. So Melinda and I curled up in bed with books, half-watching the one movie that was available on our closed-circuit TV.

Around nine o'clock the phone rang, and Melinda answered.

"That was Miss Carlisle," she told me after she hung up the phone. "The plane with Duncan's son won't be arriving until tomorrow afternoon. They're waiting for parts for an engine repair. I told her we'd go back to see Duncan tomorrow. Let's see how he's doing, and if he's okay, then we'll do some sightseeing. Okay?"

"Sounds good. Sweet dreams."

"I wish."

CRUISE DAY SIX

FRIDAY

CHAPTER THIRTEEN

SUPER HEROES

We didn't see any of our cruise mates at breakfast the next day either. I was a little upset with them for not finding us and, at least, asking how Duncan was. I was also surprised that Sylvia hadn't wanted to visit Duncan and stake her claim on the potential widower. Melinda sloughed it off. I was glad they weren't my friends. I'd be very offended if they'd forgotten about me so quickly.

After breakfast, the ship's customer service representative called us a taxi. As we sped through the streets, I made a point of noticing the palm trees that lined both sides and the dingy, pastel cottages crouched behind overgrown, unkempt bushes. Trash bins and old appliances sat on the lawns.

What we could see of Charlotte Amalie was not especially pretty, but I would have liked to have seen some of the nicer neighborhoods or, perhaps, taken an eco-tour of the forests. Would there be time after Duncan's son arrived? And what if something else happened to Justin's flight and he *didn't* arrive? The ship would be leaving at five this evening. Would we even be on board?

Once again we wound our way through the labyrinthine corridors of the Roy Lester Schneider Hospital to Duncan's room on the fourth floor. We turned a corner and were shocked at what we found.

Duncan was hanging onto the railing on the side of his hospital bed—looking haggard and panic-stricken, sweat pouring off his forehead—and gasping for breath. I immediately burst into tears; I thought we were watching him die. On our heels, the nurse arrived with a mask that she thrust over his face, strapped onto the back of his head, and attached to a nearby machine. She turned to the machine, which was sitting on a metal cart, to adjust the dials. The dials appeared to be regulating the airflow. An aide came in to help Duncan while the nurse spoke to us. Duncan's panic appeared to subside.

"He's having problems again," the nurse explained. "This apparatus is a nebulizer. It will pump oxygen and medicine into Mr. Blumen's lungs."

A man in green scrubs arrived and took over for the aide.

"I'm the respiratory therapist, Dr. Eckert," he introduced himself. "We're trying very hard to keep Mr. Blumen from being intubated."

"What's that?" I asked.

"We don't want to have to put him on a respirator," the nurse explained. "Once that happens, he can't leave. He has to stay here on the island until he's healthy enough to travel home, and we have no idea how many days or weeks that might take. We're not set up here to take care of people with Mr. Blumen's health problems. I've put in a call to his travel insurance company to explain the situation. Do you know when his son will arrive?"

"The ship's liaison said this afternoon. His plane was delayed in San Juan."

"We'll do our best to keep him off the respirator," Dr. Eckert said.

Melinda and I sat down on two metal folding chairs in one corner of the room. The nurse continued to talk to us.

"Mr. Blumen is very frightened, which doesn't help his condition. The medicine in the nebulizer is albuterol, which can cause anxiety. When we treated him last night, he became upset, so we had to give him some morphine to settle him down."

We heard a slap and turned to see the respiratory therapist pounding Duncan on the back with the open palm of his hand.

"What's he doing?" I asked in alarm.

"Trying to get the old air out of the patient's lungs. He can't breathe in oxygen until the carbon dioxide is expelled."

We watched helplessly as the RT encouraged Duncan to take deep breaths in and out, slowly forcing oxygen into his lungs. Every so often he slapped him on the back again, which caused Duncan to gasp as he exhaled.

"What exactly is his diagnosis?" I asked the nurse.

"He suffers from COPD and congestive heart disease," she answered. "Other than that, I can't tell you anything."

"Do you know his wife is missing?" Melinda said. "That also explains why he's so easily upset."

"Thank you," she replied. "We didn't know. I think that does explain a lot about his mental state. And the moisture in this tropical air doesn't help either. He's exactly the wrong person in the wrong place at the wrong time."

Melinda and I were too worried even to read our books. We took turns going for walks up and down the corridors, visiting the tearoom for coffee and, eventually, lunch. I was afraid to leave Duncan alone even with the medical staff. I felt it was important that someone he knew be with him at all times. I wasn't a clairsentient like Melinda, but I felt very strongly that he could die here.

It was a long day. The RT rarely left the room. Duncan became upset around two in the afternoon, and the nurse gave him a shot of something called Ativan®. She told us it would calm him down. It made him sleepy and disoriented. He napped, but fifteen minutes later, he woke up in a panic, not knowing where he was.

The nurse spoke softly to him and calmed him down.

"You're okay, Mr. Blumen," she said. "Your friends are here, and your son is on his way. You have nothing to worry about."

"Phoebe!" he gasped. "I have to find Phoebe!"

Melinda stood up and walked over to him. She took hold of his right hand, which she later told me was disturbingly cold. She rubbed his hand back and forth between both of hers, trying to rub a little warmth back into it.

"We're still looking for her," she reassured him. "Everyone on the ship is looking for her. Try not to worry. We'll find her."

I knew he wasn't going to stop worrying. I also knew we might not find her, but what else could Melinda say to a husband in such extreme distress?

All through the afternoon, the RT encouraged Duncan to breathe deeply in and out. At one point Duncan reared up with a wild look in his eyes, gasping again, unable to catch a breath. This time the RT put a different sort of mask on his face and told us that it was a CPAP mask, something that would force air down into Duncan's lungs. He said it was his last resort before intubation.

Wrinkled black tubing projected from a hard plastic mask that encompassed Duncan's nose and mouth and hooked him up to a rumbling bedside machine; poor Duncan looked like a bizarre alien from a science fiction movie. I was half-tempted to take a photo so I could show it to every teenager I met to prove what the probable results of years of smoking were. I didn't; it would have been in incredibly poor taste. But I couldn't help thinking that such a picture might frighten just a few preteens as they reached for their first cigarette.

Sometime in the late afternoon, Duncan began to breathe normally again. The RT removed the CPAP mask, replacing it with only the oxygen tubes, and took a much-deserved break, leaving us alone. Duncan seemed clear-headed and, looking at us with an appreciative smile, said, "Thank you for staying. Is Justin here yet?"

"He'll be here soon," Melinda told him. "It looks like it was touch and go there for a while."

"The staff here is unbelievable," Duncan said. "I owe them my life. But Phoebe isn't here. Is there any news?"

"No, I'm sorry, there isn't."

I braced myself for another bout of breathing problems and looked around for the nurse, but I guess the medications were doing their job. Duncan remained calm and relaxed, breathing comfortably with only the oxygen tubes running into his nose.

When the nurse returned she said she had spoken to the company that handled Duncan's trip insurance. He had been cleared to be medevacked to a mainland hospital immediately, probably the Cleveland Clinic in Florida. A team would come around four o'clock to prepare him. I sincerely hoped his son would have arrived by then.

Melinda called Miss Carlisle and asked what time the ship would be leaving for St. Kitts, the next stop on our cruise. When Melinda hung up the phone she said, with a worried look, that the ship was scheduled to leave at five, but given the circumstances they would wait for us until six o'clock. If we weren't back by then, the ship would sail without us.

At four thirty, three strangers appeared, one man and two women. They wore silver jump suits with red badges on their chests and wide red belts. They carried bulging leather duffel bags. They stood in front of us with their feet spread apart and their hands on their hips, looking for all the world like superheroes come to Duncan's rescue.

"This is Mr. Duncan Blumen?" the man asked?

"Yes," the nurse replied.

"I'm Dr. Stewart," he said. "And this is my team, Ms. Reynolds and Ms. Gavatos. They are licensed EMTs. We are here to take Mr. Blumen to Fort Lauderdale."

He continued in a flat voice, "Our Learjet is being readied. An ambulance is waiting downstairs to take the patient to the airfield, but first we need to examine him and prepare him for travel."

After an exchange of paperwork and signatures, the nurse began to assist the team with Duncan's prep. Melinda and I sat motionless in wonder as the four people replaced floor-model IVs and monitors with portable ones. They were quiet and efficient, moving in tune with one another like dancers in a pantomime as they went gracefully about their duties. We were so entranced at their performance that we didn't notice the young man who appeared at the door and suddenly said "Is this Duncan Blumen's room? I'm his son, Justin."

"Thank God," I said, right out loud.

To our surprise, Duncan was able to sit up and smile. Justin went up to his father and kissed him on the forehead.

"What's happening with my dad?" he asked.

The doctor explained that he was being medevacked to the Cleveland Clinic on the mainland.

"But I just got here." Justin was tall, thin, and wearing the casual uniform of all men of means—a dark golf shirt and crisp khakis. He had the thinning brown hair of his dad along with his round, smooth face. He carried a small overnight bag and seemed uncomfortable with not being the one giving orders.

"You can come with us," Dr. Stewart said. "There's just enough room in the jet."

"Have they found Phoebe?" Justin asked Melinda.

"No, I'm sorry. There's no news," she replied.

"I'm sure that doesn't help his condition," Justin frowned.

"No, I'm sure it doesn't," Melinda responded.

We never got a chance to say good-bye to Duncan. Like Cinderella's coachman and footmen, the team suddenly whisked Duncan and his hospital bed away down the corridor with Justin trailing behind. Justin looked back at us once, with an apologetic look on his face like he was sorry he hadn't spoken to us more. I was just grateful he had arrived.

A few minutes later, as Melinda and I were leaving, we saw Dr. Eckert talking to the nurses at their station. He stopped when he saw us and came over.

"You don't know how close you came to losing your friend," he said. "He's seriously ill."

"We were already read the riot act by the doctor on the cruise ship about us old folks traveling when we have medical conditions," I said. "But it was his honeymoon."

"And where's his wife?"

"Missing," Melinda said.

"Well, they'll be in my prayers," he replied and returned to the nurses.

We flagged a taxi at the entrance to the hospital and took it back to the ship. We got there at exactly 5:45, fifteen minutes before the ship was scheduled to sail.

"How about a drink?" Melinda suggested.

"I could use one," I replied, sighing with relief at being back on board.

We went up to deck thirteen and were glad to find a bar open. We got drinks from the jazz club and went outside to enjoy the warm summer evening. We headed toward some empty tables with plastic chairs along the outer walkway. Just as we sat down, we felt the ship pull away from the dock.

CHAPTER FOURTEEN
The Lovely Casandra

"What a day!" Melinda exclaimed. "I'm so relieved Justin got there. I hated to see Duncan taken away by strangers to a hospital he's not familiar with and where he has no friends."

"I agree. I really was afraid he was going to die."

"They would have put him on a respirator before that could happen."

"I know, but given his heart issues and Phoebe missing, I think he could have had a heart attack or a stroke at any moment. Remind me to get a doctor's letter from the next man I date. No smoking, no COPD, no heart issues, no diabetes, and no alcoholism."

"Get used to being single."

"I guess I'll have to."

As we sat and enjoyed our drinks, we idly watched couples come and go along the deck, some holding hands, some chatting, and some softly arguing. Party lights twinkled along lengthy wires looped between the masts. A live band was performing at the jazz club; their mellow horns gave an other-worldly feel to the softness of the evening.

Out of the shadows, a couple with arms wrapped tightly around each other's waists drifted into sight.

Melinda sat up and pointed to them when they got closer and became easier to see.

I watched them, and although there was some light coming from inside the club, it was still difficult to discern their faces. It looked to me like Sylvia with Sven. That was a shock, but then again, why not. I'm sure she was hoping to meet someone special on the cruise. Unfortunately, this someone would be sailing on without her five days from now.

"Hey!" Melinda suddenly called out. "Sylvia!"

The couple turned to face us and looked surprised to see us there. "How's Duncan?" Sylvia asked.

"Being medevacked to Fort Lauderdale," Melinda said. "Any word on Phoebe?"

"No. We understand the Coast Guard has been on board and conducted their own search. They didn't find anything. The captain said there's nothing more he can do."

"You all know Sven," she said, doing the introductions a bit late.

"Of course," I smiled.

"We're going to eat in the steak house after the show tonight so I won't be at the table for dinner."

"I think dinner's already started," Melinda said, looking at her watch. "Have fun."

They wandered away again, and I felt just a twinge of annoyance that Sven would be dining with Sylvia instead of me. Had Sylvia set out to snake him away from me, or had Sven sought her out? I would probably never know.

"Let's grab something to eat in the casual dining room," Melinda suggested, and we headed down to deck twelve.

As Melinda and I ate, we watched St. Thomas retreat from view. I was sorry we'd never gotten to tour the island, but I don't know what else we could have done. With Phoebe missing, someone had to stay with Duncan. Melinda wouldn't have minded if I'd left her alone and did some sightseeing, but what kind of a friend would do that?

"We haven't seen Jane and Rick," Melinda remarked. "What do you suppose happened after Wednesday night's séance?"

"They were doing so well," I replied. "I hope this news about Phoebe and the baby didn't cause a major rift."

"Perhaps they decided to spend another day or two in the sack," Malinda said, smiling at her thoughts.

"More power to them. I'll have to remember that the next time I get married."

"You'd marry again?" Melinda asked, surprised. She knew how difficult my recovery from divorce had been ten years ago and about my recent breakup with Bud.

"Sure, I'd risk it, and now I have Jane and Rick's formula for success. If they could only help me find a marriageable guy."

Melinda gave a little snort of amusement and we let the matter drop.

As we were deciding on dessert, Liz appeared.

"I seem to have been forgotten," she said. "There was no one at our table, so I ate by myself. What have you two been up to?"

Liz sat down while Melinda described how we'd stayed with Duncan until his son and the medevac team had arrived. He was now on his way to the Cleveland Clinic in Florida.

"Well, I'm glad he'll be taken care of," she said, but she frowned, like she wasn't glad at all.

"What did you do today?" I asked her.

"Sylvia and I took a catamaran tour of the island. It was fun. The sun was brilliant and the ocean was calm. We really sped over the water. After that, we stopped at a beach for lunch and snorkeling."

"Do you both snorkel?" I asked her. I was struggling with a vision of Sylvia in mask and fins.

"Sylvia doesn't but I do. The reefs were astonishing. I even caught a glimpse of an endangered green sea turtle."

"What did Jane and Rick do?"

"They said they were going to the beach. I was glad to hear that. I was worried they would be fighting after what happened at the séance."

"We just saw Sylvia with Sven, the cruise director. How did that happen?" I was glad Melinda asked the question, because I couldn't have without sounding as if I cared.

"He was on our catamaran excursion with us. He said he was doing research. Sylvia went out of her way to be charming and humorous. It worked." Liz's tone of voice said that she wasn't too pleased about that either.

"Any more word about Phoebe?" I asked.

"No, sorry. We saw Miss Carlisle when we returned to the ship; she said there was no news. But I do want to tell you something else I remembered about Duncan. It might be useful."

"What?" Melinda and I said in unison.

"When Phoebe first started dating him, she told me that she was concerned about his past. Seems his first wife had taken out a restraining order against him when they separated. Phoebe was concerned he might have violent tendencies. She never spoke of it again, and I didn't ask."

"Have you ever seen him angry?" I asked.

"No, I haven't," she looked thoughtful. "And I've seen him deal with some very stressful situations at the hospital."

"Did Phoebe ever seem afraid of Duncan?" I inquired.

"Oh no," Liz replied. "Never."

"People request those protection orders for all kinds of reasons during a nasty divorce," Melinda suggested. "He could have just left an angry message on her answering machine because she canceled a visitation with the kids, and she overreacted."

"Well, I hope that's all it was," I said. The other two nodded their heads in agreement.

"There's a magic show in the auditorium at seven thirty," Liz said. "Do you guys want to go?"

"Sure, let's do that," I said. Melinda agreed. "We'll skip dessert and get something sweet and alcoholic to drink."

"Good idea," I said, and off we three went to the show.

As we sat on soft chairs and enjoyed our margaritas, Jane and Rick entered. We waved for them to join us. Both were smiling and tan. They sat down at once and told us what a great time they'd had at the beach, named, romantically enough, Honeymoon Beach.

"They go all out on these excursions," Rick said. "Free rumrunners, tons of food, towels, beach chairs, umbrellas...they didn't miss anything. These are the most beautiful beaches I've ever seen."

"It's one of the nicest days we've ever spent together," Jane said. They had obviously smoothed over the events of the séance. It renewed my faith in the institution of marriage to see a couple deal with a problem and then move on. Or, at least, I hoped they'd moved on. There was always a chance that it had just been dismissed and then hidden away, only to become one more weapon in a morbidly cherished arsenal of hurts that could be deployed at the next big blowup.

"How's Duncan?" Jane finally thought to ask, and Melinda updated them on Justin's arrival, the medevac team, and their flight to Florida.

"I'm so glad his son arrived," Jane said when Melinda was done. "He shouldn't be alone."

As I looked around the auditorium, I noticed Alastair and his girlfriend wander in and sit down four of five rows up from us. The girlfriend looked younger than any of us. She had honey blonde hair fluffed out around her head and cascading down onto her shoulders. She also had a curvy figure that she set off with a low cut white sweater and skintight red mini skirt. Everyman's

Barbie® Doll, I thought unkindly. Alastair was dressed in a tuxedo; I wondered what that was about.

Rick saw the couple and quickly looked away. He wasn't going to spoil Jane's good mood by pointing them out. I mentally praised him for his common sense. He might be that rare man who understood the effect beautiful women have on those of us not so blessed.

I spoke softly to Melinda, "Given what you've told me about Alastair's shaky finances, how did he attract a gorgeous woman like Casandra?"

"I heard that his father died and left him half a million," she replied.

"He should be able to afford the alimony then."

"I don't know. Half a mil isn't what it used to be. Oh, there's Elvis!" Melinda waved as he appeared in the auditorium doorway and continued down the aisle toward us. We all moved our chairs around to accommodate one more. Melinda introduced him to us all, and again I couldn't quite figure out his last name. It seemed to have lots of *g*'s and *d*'s and *k*'s. For just a second, I considered that his name was probably Slavic. Could he have been one of the gentlemen seen dancing with Phoebe that night?

As Elvis greeted each of us, the lights dimmed and the audience quieted down. Sven appeared on the stage. He introduced Siobhan, who would be singing some songs from her new album. I was surprised to see someone I'd already heard on the radio.

"Pretty good talent for a cruise ship," I whispered to Melinda. "Does she get a free cruise?"

"I doubt it. She probably got on in St. Thomas and is getting off in St. Kitts."

Siobhan began to sing a medley of old Irish ballads about love, death, and ghostly children. She was tall and slender, with silky straight hair and pale skin. Dressed in a floor length gown of deep blue, she looked a bit like a wraith herself. There was a young man in peasant garb accompanying her on guitar. For her last song, a flutist came on stage and interspersed the verses with his ethereal piping. We were all enchanted and applauded like crazy when it was over.

Next came the magician who turned out to be Alastair. We all looked at each other in surprise. "Did you know he was an amateur magician?" I whispered to Melinda. She shook her head.

Alastair performed a few card tricks, pulled the traditional rabbit from a hat, and produced scarves from thin air. For his next trick, he called upon "Casandra, the lovely young lady sitting in aisle fourteen," to join him. His girlfriend stood up and walked up to the stage. He directed her to stand against a large black board and hold her arms out perpendicular to her body. She looked very beautiful and vulnerable, like a proper magician's assistant should. Alastair picked up six large knives.

"Let's hope he misses," Liz whispered.

A drumroll began as he showed the knives to the audience. The steel blades caught the glint of the spotlight and shimmered with peril. As he aimed his first knife, the audience as a whole breathed in; you could feel their nervous excitement.

Thwack! The first knife landed inches from Casandra's outer right thigh. Alastair turned to the audience and gave a short bow. He turned back to his girlfriend. Another thwack! The second knife landed inches from her outer left thigh. Alastair paused for another short bow and turned immediately back to his task. As he aimed his third, the audience together breathed in a soft "Ohhh!" Then, thwack! The third knife lodged itself under Casandra's right arm pit. Another short bow to the audience. Thwack! The fourth landed under her left arm pit.

The astonished "Ohhh!" was louder now. Alastair took another bow. I put my hands in front of my face; I couldn't look at where the next knife would be aimed. Thwack! With my eyes covered, I heard the fifth knife hit the board. I peeked out between my fingers to see it lodged just inches from Casandra's right ear. Before I knew what was happening and without Alastair's stopping for a bow this time, there was a final thwack! I gasped along with the crowd, as the sixth knife found a home in a tuft of hair on the upper left side of Casandra's head. We all breathed out a chorus of "No!" as we waited for the blood to begin spurting. But there was no blood, only a very pale Casandra. The audience burst into applause.

Casandra freed her hair from the blade and pulled herself away from the board. She wobbled just a bit as Alastair ran to take her hand. He didn't appear to be upset by how close he'd come to hurting her. He raised her hand in his, and they stood there together with arms held high enjoying the moment.

"Close call there," Liz said. "I'd never let that man throw knives at me."

"Me neither," I agreed. "Although it's the danger that makes it so exciting."

"She wasn't really in danger," Rick said. "It's all an act. Something to do with magnets."

"Still...a pretty convincing performance," asserted Elvis.

As the applause died down, Alastair addressed the audience.

"My gorgeous assistant, you will agree, has been a tremendous good sport. I think she deserves a reward." As he spoke the last few words, he pulled out a small white box and got down on one knee, facing Casandra. She reacted with a frown. Perhaps this wasn't part of the act.

"Darling," he said after kissing her hand. "Will you marry me?"

The audience loved it. Everyone jumped up from their seats and starting stomping their feet and clapping their hands. "Say yes!" they shouted, over and over again until the lovely Casandra smiled and appeared to say "Yes." You couldn't hear for sure over the noise of the crowd.

Alastair began to slip the ring on Casandra's left ring finger. He appeared to be having some difficulty and had to push extra hard to get it over the knuckle. Casandra grimaced but quickly recovered and held her hand out so that the gem caught the spotlight. The diamond was a good size, maybe one and a half or two carats, and there was no mistaking the sparkle.

The crowd continued clapping for another ten seconds, and then the applause slowly died.

"That bastard," Jane murmured as we rose to leave. "He risked her life just to show off."

"Well, I'm beat," Melinda said, changing the topic. "I'm off to bed."

"Time for one more drink?" Elvis asked her.

"Of course. Em, see you later."

"No problem."

We joined the throng of people clogging the aisles.

"See you in the morning," Jane said as the momentum of the crowd carried us up the aisle. "We wake up in St. Kitts."

I returned to our cabin alone, glad for some time to myself.

Later that night, after Melinda returned and was getting undressed, she said, "I'm surprised that Alastair gave Casandra a ring tonight. I mean, where did he get it? We're on a cruise to St. Kitts, where you can buy jewelry so much cheaper than anywhere in the United States. If I were getting engaged, I'd have bought a ring in

St. Kitts. Oh well, maybe he bought it before he booked the cruise. Or he could have bought it on St. Thomas."

"I didn't know jewelry was cheaper in St. Kitts," I replied. "Maybe he didn't either. How was your date with Elvis?"

"We had a wonderful time. We went dancing up on deck thirteen in the disco bar."

"Mel, I hate to say this, but it has occurred to me that his last name sounded Slavic. Do you think he was one of the gentleman seen dancing with Phoebe?"

"I doubt it. He told me he was seasick for the first two or three days until he broke down and got some medication from the infirmary."

"Please be careful, though."

"Of course! Now...nighty-night."

CRUISE DAY SEVEN

SATURDAY

CHAPTER FIFTEEN

Basseterre

The phone rang shortly after midnight. Startled from a deep sleep, I leapt out of bed and ran to the desk. I fumbled for the lamp, turned it on, and quickly answered it. "Who's this?" I barked, annoyed at being awoken.

"It's Miss Carlisle," said a soft, worried voice. "I'm afraid I have very bad news. The plane carrying Mr. Blumen and his son to the mainland never arrived in Fort Lauderdale. At dawn, search planes will be sent out to look for survivors and debris. That's all I know as of now. I'll call you as soon as I hear anything more."

"Have you told the other members of our party?" I managed to ask, although I was almost too stunned to speak.

"Yes. I called the Smiths first, then Miss Marsh and Miss Spode. You were my last call."

"Thank you," I said and replaced the receiver.

I woke up Melinda and told her the bad news.

"I can't believe this is happening," she moaned. She turned on her side, facing me, and brought her knees up to her chest in the fetal position. She clutched her extra pillow in her arms in front of her. I could see tears forming in her eyes.

"First Phoebe, and now Duncan and his son," she said. "With his health problems, Duncan could never survive a plane crash. He was probably strapped to the gurney so he wouldn't roll around during the flight. He'd be trapped. How awful!"

The picture in my mind's eye of the plane crash and its subsequent sinking was horrific, with a gasping Duncan struggling to free himself from his bonds as water flooded the Learjet's cabin. His son would have made a desperate attempt to aid him. I said a silent prayer that somehow they would be found alive.

Melinda buried her head in the pillow she was holding. "Oh

no, no, no! This can't be," she moaned again and started to sob
in earnest.

"Shall I call the others? Do you think we should get together?"
I asked, going over to sit on her bed and rub her shoulders, trying
to soothe her.

"No. If they call us, we can go to their rooms, but let's stay here
for now. I'm really too upset to talk to them."

We sat there in quiet grief for another half an hour. Poor
Duncan, and his son might be lost also. What a devastating blow for
their family.

Melinda didn't want to talk, and I didn't start any conversations.
Around two, it looked like Melinda had fallen back to sleep. Since
there was nothing else to do, I shut off the light and went to sleep
myself, worn out from worry.

When we awoke later in morning, Melinda and I said little as
we washed and dressed. When I glanced out the balcony doors,
I saw that we were docked in St Kitts.

We went up to deck twelve for breakfast and found our
remaining cruise mates together at a table—everyone, except for
Liz. When I asked where she was, Sylvia said, "She was gone when
I woke up. I guess she's power walking."

At hearing this, Melinda gave her an odd look, then said,
"You've all heard about Duncan and his son."

"Yes," Rick said for himself and Jane. He didn't add anything.
They were both pale, probably from grief and lack of sleep.

"I can't believe it!" Jane suddenly wailed. "It's like we're cursed.
Is this the Flying Dutchman? Can we get off and go home?"

"That's a thought," Melinda said. "We've just docked in St.
Kitts. I'm sure they have an airport if you seriously want to leave."

"Maybe we should consider that," Rick replied. "But I think the
runway on St. Kitts is too small for jumbo jets. We'd have to take an
island hopper and go to another island, maybe Puerto Rico. There
we'd have to book a flight back to the mainland. There might not be
anything today or tomorrow."

"And it would be awfully expensive, hon," Jane added.

"So I guess we should stay here," Rick concluded. "But I don't
want to sit here all day and stew in my worry and grief. Shall we
keep the plans we made?"

He told the rest of us that they'd already booked an excursion
to explore Basseterre city.

"Let's take the tour," he said to his wife. "It'll take our mind off all this. There's nothing else we can do."

Jane agreed. "What will the rest of you do? Want to join us on the tour?"

Sylvia said she was going to look for Liz, and maybe, they'd go ashore and wander through the town, do some shopping. Jane and Rick silently piled their dishes on a tray and left.

Melinda and I lingered over our coffee and discussed going ashore. Then we saw Sven striding across the dining room. He came straight to our table and sat down.

"I'm very sorry," Sven said, taking a seat and looking concerned. "This hasn't been a pleasant cruise for you and your friends. I hope you don't think any of this is the fault of our ship or crew."

"No, of course not," I replied. "Let's just hope nothing else happens."

Melinda was looking ill again and said nothing. Even though I hardly knew the book club members, I had spent enough time with them by now to be terribly upset. I could imagine how much more distressing it was for Melinda. I thought of Jane's lament about a curse and had to agree with her.

"Thank you, Sven," I said and didn't say anything further. I didn't want to be chatting with him while Melinda wasn't feeling well. He took the hint and excused himself, promising he would update us with any news.

"What do you want to do?" I asked Melinda. "We don't have to go into the town."

"No, let's," she replied. "There's nothing we can do, and I can't just sit here. All we seem to do on this cruise is sit and worry."

We went back to our stateroom and got ready to leave. As we descended to the main deck, Melinda's shoulders drooped and she hung her head. I knew she was struggling with her feelings, both her own and the extrasensory perception of the feelings of others. Such knowledge is often of little help.

As we disembarked, we saw that the ship was docked at the end of a long pier. It was maybe three hundred yards from the end of the pier to the island.

"Bit of a hike," I remarked, but was glad of the exercise.

As we walked, I took notice of the lush green mountains of St. Kitts rising dark and mysterious out of the sea. Mist clouds like smoke rings surrounded the peaks, and below them red tile roofs appeared as fringe where the emerald foliage tumbled down to the sea.

On the island a fleet of tour buses were waiting for excursion passengers. Smaller vans waited for anyone needing a ride around the city of Basseterre. We walked through a wide arch; on the other side, islanders had set up tables to sell jewelry and trinkets.

Further along, we walked along cobblestoned streets with restaurants and shops. The huts housing these businesses were casually built, three-sided affairs that opened onto the street. Display racks of sunglasses, postcards, beach bags, and straw hats cluttered the way. Island music flowed around us like so many gauzy scarves; the air was filled with spicy aromas and floral scents.

Melinda and I wandered through streets packed with tourists. We peered into shops, but didn't enter any. I don't think either one of us was in the mood for shopping.

At lunchtime we found a bar in a pink-and-yellow-painted wooden pavilion. We ordered jerk chicken sandwiches and the house beer. I suddenly realized there might have been fifteen or twenty minutes during the morning when I was able to forget about Phoebe and Duncan.

As we sat in silence, Sylvia wandered by all alone. She didn't look in, so she didn't see us watching her.

"I wonder where Liz is," I said.

"Don't know, don't care," Melinda lied.

I raised my glass of beer in a toast, and Melinda hoisted hers to tap mine.

"Here's to a true vacation day at last," she said, more with a feeling of hope than a firm conviction.

"May there be many more," I responded.

We spent another hour in the bar, reluctant to leave, glad to be free of the gloomy atmosphere of the ship and the riddle of Phoebe's disappearance. We ordered a second round of beer and told ourselves that we were soaking up the "island experience."

Around three o'clock boredom was setting in, so we decided to head back to the ship. Along the way we saw Melinda's friend, Elvis, sitting by himself at another bar, alone.

"What's up?" Melinda asked him as we stopped to chat.

"Just keeping an eye on everyone," he replied. "Care to join me for a beer?"

"Are you our den mother?" Melinda asked, smiling, but she didn't take a seat.

"Well, not exactly. I'm just a self-appointed observer of human nature."

"You haven't seen our friend, Liz, passing by, have you? She's the thin one with brownish hair."

"Not today," he replied.

"We're heading back to the ship," she said. "Maybe we'll see you later."

"Okay."

We waved good-bye and headed off into the late afternoon sun.

Back on board, we decided to sit by the pool for an hour or two before dinner. The ship would be leaving at five, headed for our next stop, Tortola, in the British Virgin Islands. We didn't bother to change our clothes, just found lounge chairs on the deck and put up our feet.

"Another beer?" I asked Melinda when a waiter stopped by.

"I think it's time to switch to something lighter," she said. "How about vodka and tonic?"

"Two," I said to the young man, "with a twist of lime." He hustled off with our order.

I closed my eyes and thought about napping. I heard the waiter return, but I think I dozed off before I'd even taken a sip of my drink. I was dreaming of rain forests, strapping young guides, and monkeys screeching in the trees when I suddenly awoke to hear Sylvia calmly saying "She's nowhere to be found. She's not in our stateroom, I didn't see her in St. Kitts, and she didn't sign up for an excursion. Where could she be?"

"And we're departing in half an hour," I heard Melinda say with panic edging into her voice. I opened my eyes.

"Are you talking about Liz?" I asked, sitting up.

"Yes," Sylvia said. "I haven't seen her since that awful phone call last night. When I didn't see her in the morning, I figured she was walking. When I didn't see her later, I assumed she wanted to take an excursion without me. She knows I don't snorkel or cave dive or any of that dangerous stuff. But all the excursions are back. It's four thirty. We'll be leaving soon."

"Have you seen Jane and Rick?" Melinda asked. "Maybe she's with them."

"I can't find them either."

"Let's go down to the Security checkpoint and ask the Security officers if they have a record of her leaving."

"Okay, let's do that," Sylvia agreed.

"Do you want to go, Emily, or stay here?"

"I'll stay here. If I see Liz, I'll tell her that you're looking for her."

Melinda and Sylvia left. I sat back in my chair and hoped they would find her. We'd lost enough people on this trip. What were the odds of losing another?

Then I heard angry voices from four lounge chairs away.

"It doesn't fit. I don't want it," whined a female voice.

I looked around and found the source. It was the soon-to-be wed Casandra, pulling at the diamond ring on her finger.

"Why couldn't you have bought me a ring on St. Kitts, like we planned? Where did you get this one? You didn't even ask me my ring size first."

I decided to be nosy and walked over to them.

"What a beautiful ring!" I said, glancing at the sparkling stone. "Don't worry, you can get it resized."

"That's what I told her," Alastair said, looking at me to emphasize our agreement.

"Where did you get it?" I asked him, noticing that it looked suspiciously like Phoebe's. Although princess cut diamonds are common, Phoebe's had had a circlet of diamond chips set in gold surrounding the center stone, exactly like Casandra's. The carat size also seemed similar.

"I purchased it back in New Hampshire," he said. "I had forgotten that jewelry in the Caribbean is less expensive. We'll get it resized when we get back home."

"If my finger doesn't swell and fall off first," Casandra sulked.

"It'll be fine," Alastair said. "You just can't get it back over the knuckle. We'll deal with it when we get home."

"It is gorgeous," I said, smiling innocently at them. "It reminds me a lot of Phoebe's," I added.

Casandra's eyes shot a panicked glance at mine. I think she got my hint.

Satisfied with having stirred up more trouble, I went back to my own chair. I couldn't wait to tell Melinda. Suppose it was Phoebe's? What did that mean? Had Alastair killed her so he wouldn't have to pay alimony, and did he take her ring to give to Casandra? What a psychotic cad! As I went over all the possibilities in my mind, Jane and Rick appeared, smiling and holding hands.

"You should have come with us," Rick said. "It's a beautiful city and we saw some very luxurious homes."

"You didn't happen to see Liz while you were on the island?" I asked.

"Oh no," Jane cried out. "She's not missing, is she?" She sat down abruptly on a neighboring lounge chair. Her happiness had evaporated in a nanosecond.

"No, we didn't see her," Rick said. "We haven't seen her all day. She wasn't at breakfast, as you know. We just assumed she was with Sylvia."

"When Liz didn't come back to the room, Sylvia thought maybe she had signed up for an excursion without her. Melinda and Sylvia have gone down to the Security checkpoint at the entrance to see if they logged her ID in and out. They should be back any moment."

"Could she have met a man and be staying with him in his cabin? You know...a romantic rendezvous," I asked.

"Knowing Liz, I doubt it," Jane said.

Rick found a seat and sat down. We all looked glum as we watched Melinda and Sylvia appear at the far end of the deck and weave their way through the lounge chairs down to where we sat.

"She never left the ship according to Security," Melinda said. "She must still be on board."

"We're in big time trouble with the cruise staff," Sylvia added. "They seem to think we're losing people on purpose, like it's some kind of hoax for a TV show. They gave us a hard time about our group not conforming to our profile, whatever the hell that means. They plan to leave as scheduled, which I think is in five minutes. Without evidence that Liz left the ship, they won't delay the departure."

"What do we do now?" I asked. "Search the ship all over again?"

"I'm not up to it," Jane said. "First Phoebe goes missing, then Duncan's plane goes down, and now Liz is gone. We're cursed. What's the point in trying?"

"Let's hope Liz turns up," Rick said. "Maybe she's just avoiding us because we haven't paid enough attention to her. Maybe this is all just a big pout on her part."

"It won't be the first time," Jane said. "Remember that time she didn't come to book club and wouldn't return our telephone calls or answer the door, and we ended up calling the police?"

"Yes, I do remember that," Sylvia replied. "Turned out she was fine. She said she just wasn't in the mood for company."

"And remember the time we went out to a restaurant and she didn't like the service, so without a word, she just got up, had the maître d call a taxi, and left without saying good-bye?" Melinda added.

"So we just ignore it and hope she turns up?" I asked.

Suddenly we felt the ship shudder and looked up to see St. Kitts receding from view. Melinda and I had spent such a pleasurable afternoon there. I was sorry to see the island fade into the distance.

"Even if she's nursing a hissy fit and avoiding us," Sylvia said, "I should at least see her when she returns to our stateroom to sleep tonight. I mean, where else would she sleep? I'll tell Sven to be on the lookout for her as he does his nightly strolls around the ship. Maybe I'll even offer to accompany him." Sylvia smiled as if she had a secret. It was fine by me.

"Let's go for dinner," Melinda said. "There's nothing else we can do now."

Glumly we all stood up and made our way to the elevators. As we exited the elevator on deck eight, the German band was standing there waiting to board. The woman who had spoken to me before grabbed my arm.

"Go on, I'll catch up," she said to her bandmates. "I need talk to this person."

I waved Melinda and the others on and stood waiting for the woman to speak.

"I saw something odd last night," she said to me. "You know your group is famous now on the ship. Everyone is gossiping about you. People in your party keep disappearing."

"Yes, I know. First our friend Phoebe, then her husband, now we can't find Liz...she's the thin one with brown hair."

"*Ja*, I saw her and a woman arguing. The other person was bigger than her, but I couldn't tell who it was."

"When was this?"

"Last night. My band and I were on deck twelve putting our instruments away after a midnight concert. I saw them over by the railing, and these two women were yelling at each other. I couldn't hear their voices; I could just see their bodies in angry poses. When I looked back a few minutes later, there was just the other person, looking over the side of the ship. The skinny one was gone."

"Do you think the other person pushed Liz overboard?"

"I don't know. There was enough time for the skinny one to leave, and it's not unusual for people to look over the railing at the sea below, but I thought it odd."

"Did you recognize anyone else from our party?"

"No. It was too dark."

"Did you tell Security?"

"I didn't want to start trouble. I didn't *see* anyone go overboard."

"Thank you for telling me. We'll wait to see if Liz returns to her stateroom tonight. If she doesn't, I'd like to tell Security what you just told me. Do you mind?"

"No. My name is Ariana Muller. Just tell them I'm with the German band."

"Thank you so much, Ariana. My name is Emily Menotti."

"Let me know if you find her," Ariana said. "I have to go now and meet my friends."

"Okay, I should go too."

I waved a good-bye and headed for my stateroom. When I arrived, Melinda was busy with her hair. She'd put on a long, red, flowered skirt and topped it with a creamy-toned sweater. As I changed into a lavender chiffon blouse and slinky black trousers, I told her what Ariana had said about seeing someone with Liz the night before on deck twelve.

"Who do you think it was?"

"I don't know what to think. I just can't imagine why anyone would want to harm Liz. What would be a motive?"

"Maybe she saw what happened to Phoebe. What do you think about Liz?" I asked. "Or, maybe, I should say what do you *feel* about Liz? And Jane too? Or Rick? Any clues?"

"I'm not very confident about Liz," she said. "I don't feel anything about her, which might mean she's passed on or that she's unconscious. As for Rick, he's been lying. All along I've felt he's been hiding things. Unfortunately, I can't tell what it is. Jane seems to be the only one not hiding anything. My stomach is in knots... and it's time to go to dinner."

We made our way down the long hallway to the elevator, where a crowd was already forming.

Melinda said, "Let's take the stairs. It's only three flights up."

When we arrived, there was a crowd waiting for the dining room to open. As we stood with the others, we felt the ship jolt to a stop. People began murmuring "Why are we stopping? Is there something wrong with the ship?"

Once the doors opened, the murmuring faded away as everyone made their way to their table. When Melinda and I arrived at ours we saw that we were the first to arrive. We ordered vodka martinis from Dmitri.

I asked him quickly, "Did you find out anything about our missing friend? We have someone else missing now too."

"Very sorry," he said. "My friends won't talk to me. They know that if rumors are traced to them they will lose their job."

I nodded and understood. Within a few minutes, Jane and Rick arrived, Rick looking dapper in a seersucker suit with a pale blue shirt and navy tie, and Jane resplendent in a yellow linen A-line with matching yellow heels. Despite the bad news we'd been struggling with, they were smiling and happy. Next Sylvia arrived in a black skirt and sweater set, looking dejected.

"No Liz?" Melinda asked.

"No Liz," Sylvia responded. She sat down and opened her napkin. "Let's not discuss it."

Dmitri returned with our drinks; took orders from Rick, Jane, and Sylvia; and handed round menus. As we considered our choices for the evening—sea bass, baked chicken, or pasta—Miss Carlisle appeared.

"The captain would like to speak to you later this evening," she told us. "Please meet him in the Security conference room at 11 p.m."

As she left, we felt the ship lurch and begin to move again. A voice came over the loudspeaker.

"This is your captain speaking. We are returning to the island of St. Kitts due to a sudden emergency. Do not be alarmed. There is no problem with the engines or the running of this ship. This is a matter of private investigation. It could mean a slight delay to our arrival in Tortola. I will give you more information as it becomes available. Thank you."

We sat in stunned silence as Dmitri delivered our bowls of soup. We picked up our spoons and began at once to eat as if on automatic pilot. Only Sylvia was out of rhythm. She hadn't moved at all. A gray pallor spread across her face.

"I'm not feeling well," she said and stood. "I think I've caught the Norovirus. I'll meet you all at eleven o'clock in the conference room."

My heart went out to her. She'd lost a friend, an old boyfriend, and now her best friend in the last few days. We all felt immediately crushed by the implications of the captain's announcement. In silence we finished our soup and watched as Dmitri cleared our dishes and handed out our salads. No one touched theirs.

We picked at our entrees when they arrived. Sylvia's chicken sat untouched at her place. "In case she returns" Dmitri had explained when he placed it there.

We each glanced occasionally at the empty seats for Phoebe, Duncan, and Liz. What more could go wrong?

No one felt like dessert, so we decided to kill time by going to the casino. Jane and Rick played blackjack for a while; Melinda played the slots. After fifteen minutes or so, I saw Elvis join her. I had my doubts about his sudden appearance as a newcomer to our group. I kept an eye on them as I stretched out my meager funds playing video poker. Around ten o'clock, Sven appeared at my console.

"How are you doing?" he asked. "Can I get you a drink?"

"No, I don't feel like drinking, but thank you," I said. "Do you know anything more that we do?"

"Not much. The captain's not giving the staff any information. This is highly unusual."

"Sylvia said she wanted to walk the decks with you this evening. Will you be stopping by her stateroom?"

"I already went by her stateroom. She didn't answer my knock. I didn't try a second time. I thought perhaps she wasn't in the mood for company."

So I was his second choice.

"Why don't you join me as I walk around the outside decks? Along with planning all the entertainment and excursions, it's part of my responsibilities. Can't have too many people keeping an eye on things."

I looked for Melinda but didn't see her close by. I guessed she and Elvis had gone somewhere together. I went over to where Jane and Rick were and told them I was taking a stroll with Sven.

"Emily, be careful," Jane said. "We don't know anything about him. Maybe he's responsible for Phoebe and Liz disappearing."

She had a point.

"I'll be careful," I told her and meant it.

I came back to where Sven stood and smiled at him. "All set. Let's go."

We left the casino and walked past the various shops selling clothes, jewelry, toiletries, and duty-free liquor. Seeing the duty-free shop, I asked Sven if I could bring a bottle back to my stateroom. The interesting thing about liquor on a cruise ship, he told me, was that you couldn't bring your own on board or purchase a bottle and take it to your room for personal use. If you bought it at the duty-free store, they would box it up along with your name and stateroom number and deliver it with your luggage on shore on the last day. It hardly seemed worth the trouble to me, but then, I'm not a big drinker—this cruise was an exception.

Sven and I took the elevator to deck twelve and went outside. He seemed to be heading toward the back of the ship where the lights were dimmer and the crowd thinned out. He had a large flashlight with him that he turned on and used to scan the sides of the railings and then across our path over to the corners of the deck where chairs, extra cushions, and life preservers were stored. I could picture him taking that flashlight and hitting someone on the head with it, momentarily stunning them while he lifted them up and over the railing.

Large, white, storage boxes lined the wall. The boxes were unlatched, and Sven opened the lids to each of them and shone his flashlight inside. Then I imagined him hitting someone with his flashlight, putting them in the box, and coming back later to throw them overboard. Was I next? I thought that I should be careful not to turn my back to him and planned to place my knee in his most vulnerable region if he did anything to threaten me.

"These have all been checked already by the crew," he told me, pointing to the storage units, "but I wanted to see for myself."

"There's room enough in these boxes to hide a body," I observed.

"Yes. That's why I'm looking a second time."

"Why are we heading back to St. Kitts? Does it have anything to do with Liz?"

"Yes. After we're done walking this deck, I'm supposed to accompany you down to the captain's office. He wants to speak to you."

"Just me?"

"Well, you're the logical choice. The others are all suspects."

"Suspects?"

"Of foul play, if it comes to that. You're just a friend, right? Not in the book club?"

"Yes, but how do you know that?"

"Sylvia told me."

"And you're calling the shots? Deciding who's a suspect and who's not?"

I pulled away from him, concerned that this wasn't really part of his job description. Was he putting me on? Trying to take advantage in some sick way? I also figured he was lying, because I, not being a member of the book club, was the most likely suspect.

"What exactly are your duties as a cruise director?"

"Well, most of my duties concern interactions with passengers and crew, and believe it or not, I also have clerical jobs. I do the budgeting and billing for all our activities; I plan our travel events; I keep travel logs; I host major events; and I'm responsible for reporting disputes, accidents, and injuries. The disappearance of your two friends would come under those last two categories.

"I also oversee staff and handle their reviews and evaluations. I report directly *not* to the captain, but to corporate headquarters, which is why I'm so involved in the disappearance of your friends. Along with assisting him, I need to evaluate the captain's response to each crisis and report back to corporate. The captain knows this, but he doesn't like to talk about it."

While Sven had been speaking, we'd walked our way past all the windows and doors and were now at the back of the ship. It was roughly ten thirty, and the moon was full, sitting high off the stern. Sven and I were alone in the moonlight, the sky a jewel-studded canopy. It would have been romantic if I'd thought Sven was interested in me, or if my mind hadn't been clouded with thoughts of defending myself.

"I'd like to kiss you," Sven whispered in my ear while drawing me close.

"I'm sorry, Sven, I'm just not in the mood. You are an attractive man, but I'm too worried about my friends."

I wished the circumstances could have been anything but what they were. His right arm encircled my waist and pulled me to him.

"Are you sure?"

"Yes," I said, pulling away from him. "Let's go see the captain."

"You can't win 'em all," he said lightly as he loosened his grip. "But if you change your mind, just let me know."

"I will," I promised, and I might have meant it.

Without further talk, we found our way back around to the side of the ship and in through the heavy glass doors. The German band, having just arrived, was blocking our way to the elevators. I saw Ariana with her trombone and smiled at her.

"Here for the midnight buffet?" I asked her.

"*Ja*. Will we see you there?"

"No, I have somewhere else I have to be."

Ariana looked at Sven and winked at me.

"I understand."

"No, no, not *that*," I laughed. "I have to see the captain."

"Good idea," she said. "Start at the top." Then she chuckled at her own joke.

"Do you know them?" Sven asked as we entered the elevator.

"Just Ariana. We've spoken a few times. They're on deck twelve almost every night, as I'm sure you know. They seem like a good resource for what goes on up there."

"Righto. I should have thought of that." He paused for a moment as if making a mental note to speak to the band later.

When we got to the conference room, Captain Bonaparte was on the phone. Sven and I sat quietly in leather chairs as we waited for him to finish. When he hung up, he turned to me and said, "I need your help."

"What can I do?" I replied.

"The Coast Guard at St. Kitts has informed me that they've got the body of a woman who was brought in last night by the owner of a small yacht. They found her floating in the water. She's dead. However, she had no ID, so they don't know her name. Would you go to the hospital and look at her? She might be your missing friend."

"Liz or Phoebe?"

"Either one...maybe neither. You tell me. That's why we're returning to St. Kitts. Take a look at the woman, and then let me know immediately. Here's my card with my personal line. Either you or Sven should call me when you've ascertained if the body is one of our missing passengers."

"Can I take Melinda with me?"

Sven and the captain exchanged glances. Surely Melinda couldn't be a suspect?

After hesitating a moment, Captain Bonaparte said, "Yes, it's okay. Sven will call your room as soon as we dock."

"What about the Smiths and Sylvia Marsh?"

"They should be here shortly, and I'll explain what has happened."

"I'll go find Melinda now," I said and rose to leave.

"I'm staying here," Sven said. "You stay in your stateroom, and I'll call you when we've docked. It should be in about an hour."

"Okay, see you later," I told him. I rushed out of the conference room and back to the elevators. When I got to our stateroom, I was glad to see Melinda brushing her teeth.

"Bad news," I told her. "They found a woman in the water near St. Kitts. She's at the hospital there. The captain is taking the ship back to the island, and he wants us to look at her and see if it's Phoebe or Liz."

"Is she dead?"

"Yes, I'm afraid so."

"But it might not be Phoebe or Liz?"

"That's right." Melinda shook her head with a sad frown.

To pass the time until Sven's call, we chatted and watched an old Mel Gibson flick on TV. We didn't speculate about the body we were to view. I was already exhausted with worry. I didn't want to waste any more emotional energy on wondering who it could be when it could very well be a stranger.

"Where did you and Elvis sneak off to this evening?" I asked.

"Just for a walk around the deck. Keep your fingers crossed this isn't just another shipboard romance."

Around midnight, the phone finally rang. At the same time, I felt the ship shudder to a halt.

When I said "Hello," it was Sven on the line.

"We're here," he said. "I'll meet you at the Security checkpoint."

"Of course, see you there."

Sven had changed from his dark suit into khakis and a white shirt. As the Security personnel scanned our badges, he told us he'd already called a cab. We still had to hoof it down the long pier, which we did in silence. I was so agitated that I was already sweating by the time we got to the cab, even though the temperature was in the low seventies. Sven held the door for us as Melinda and I climbed into the back.

Sven got in the front and said merely, "Hospital."

We wound through the dark lanes of the silent town and arrived at Joseph N. France General Hospital, a one story white structure with green trim. The driver followed the signs to the Emergency entrance. As we exited the cab, Sven asked the driver to wait for us. We went to the reception desk where Sven explained to the nurse on duty why we were there. She asked us to wait a moment while she called the doctor in charge.

It only took a moment before a white-coated gentleman appeared and introduced himself as Doctor Lafitte. As we followed him down the corridors, he went on to describe the hospital's services and facilities. I wondered why he was telling us all this when we already knew we were viewing a dead woman. I guess he just needed to make conversation.

The doctor took us to a corner room that required a badge to enter. After Dr. Lafitte opened the door, we all filed in to see a female form lying on a gurney with a sheet covering the entire length of the body. The body was thin, which meant it could be either Liz or Phoebe. The doctor reached up and pulled the sheet down across her chest.

The smooth, relaxed expression on the woman's face seemed at odds with her disheveled, silver-streaked brown hair. Her face was blessedly free of fish-nibbling injuries, so I figured she must have been found fairly soon after she went into the water. She looked more like an aging princess, fast asleep. The quietness of her repose reminded me of a scene from a fairy tale, the maiden awaiting her prince's kiss.

Melinda spoke to Sven softly, "Yes, this is our friend Liz Spode."

"You'll need to speak to someone in admissions and give her all the information you have," the doctor responded.

"As the ship's representative, I'll contact her next of kin," Sven said. "She would have supplied that with her reservation."

Melinda started to say something, perhaps offering to contact them instead, but then thought better of it.

"Let someone in an official capacity do this," I said in an undertone. "Her relatives might have questions we can't answer."

The doctor covered Liz back up. We left the room and returned, the way we had come, to the hospital entrance.

I waited in the lobby, pacing back and forth, as Melinda and Sven went into an office behind the reception desk. I could hear the soft cadences of voices. I figured Sven would take care of calling the captain.

As I waited, I said a few prayers for Liz's soul and worried that someone in our party was a serial killer. It didn't make sense to me, though, that a person would start a crime spree out of the blue. Didn't these psychopaths start with one murder and then wait weeks or months for the next one? And, if it were someone in our party, what clues was I missing to their identity?

When Melinda and Sven came out twenty minutes later, we all shook hands with Dr. Lafitte and thanked him for his help. The cab we had come in was waiting for us beneath the porte cochere.

"To the ship," Sven told him as we got in.

"I'm very sorry about your friend," Sven said as we drove through town. "We'll be reexamining the Security camera footage for any indication that she fell or was pushed overboard. Do you know anything you haven't shared?"

My recent encounter with Ariana flashed through my mind, but I still considered Sven a suspect. I didn't answer his question.

"I don't think so," Melinda said. "This business with Phoebe... and now Liz...has me suspecting all my book club friends. I hate thinking that one of them would harm another. You don't think it could be some anonymous passenger who's just targeting our group?"

"I don't know what to think," Sven said.

I silently agreed.

"And they still might both be accidents," he added.

Neither Melinda nor I replied to that, lost in our thoughts and wondering what the effect of Liz's death would have on the others. This vacation had turned from a fun outing into a medieval ordeal to be suffered and endured.

Melinda started to cry; a slow trickle of tears dripped down her pale cheeks. In an attempt to comfort her, I put my arm around her shoulders and touched her head with mine as we walked back to the ship. I prayed that nothing else would go wrong.

When we were back on board, Sven left us. Melinda and I went to Jane and Rick's stateroom first. They were dressed for bed but had been waiting to hear from us. Melinda gave them the bad news about Liz, and I told them what Ariana had seen on the deck. I kept an eye on Rick as I spoke to see his reaction. He had only flinched a bit when Melinda told them about identifying the body and didn't say anything.

"This can't be happening," Jane moaned, bending forward and putting her face in her hands. "How could my friends be hurt like this? Who could be capable of this? It has to be a stranger...not one of us."

Rick offered no answer. He put his arms around Jane and drew her close, trying to soothe her. "I just want this cruise to be over," he finally said.

"Oh yes, please...I wish we could just go home," Jane moaned. Then she turned to Melinda and me. "Did you tell the captain what that woman saw?" Jane asked.

"No, not yet," I replied. "She didn't actually see anyone push Liz over the railing. We can't be one hundred percent sure that's what happened. I'm waiting to see if the Security videos show anything."

"We better go tell Sylvia about Liz," Melinda said. We left Jane and Rick and went next door. When we knocked, the door was immediately opened by Sven. He had obviously come straight to Sylvia's room. He didn't say anything, just held the door wide so Melinda and I could enter. Sylvia lay on her bed sobbing.

Melinda sat beside her and spoke in a comforting tone, "We're so sorry, Sylvia. I know she was your best friend."

"Now I don't have Duncan or Liz," she said, choking on her words. "What am I going to do? What am I going to *do*?"

"We're all in this together," Melinda said soothingly. "We'll figure it out. You're not alone."

With nothing else to say, Melinda and I left. Sven closed the door behind us.

"Do you think she's safe with just Sven there?" I asked. "He could be the one responsible. We don't know who he is. What better place for a homicidal maniac to hide than on a cruise ship? You can see how indifferent the captain and his staff are to all these disappearances."

"I don't think its Sven," she said. "He's just your garden variety Romeo. But you're right that it could be a stranger who's targeted us."

"Then what can we do?"

"I don't know. Just wait, I guess. And keep alert."

Back in our room, we changed into nightclothes and sank into our beds, exhausted from the long day and late night. My mind was filled with a raging storm of thoughts about how vulnerable we all were to unexplained violence.

"I'd say 'sweet dreams' but I very much doubt that'll happen," I said as I switched off the light.

"I'll be happy if they're just not nightmares," Melinda replied.

I don't think either one of us fell asleep right away. I lay there in the dark trying to think of a motive for anyone to kill

Phoebe and Liz. I couldn't come up with one. Eventually, I was lulled to sleep by the rocking movement of the ship.

CRUISE DAY EIGHT

SUNDAY

CHAPTER SIXTEEN

MOUNT SAGE

When I awoke on Sunday, I realized I had been on this cruise for one week. So much had transpired that it felt like a full year. Friends had suffered and friends had died; hopes had been raised and hopes had been dashed; the sun had risen and the sun had set, bringing more bad news with it each day. I was ready for this adventure to be over and to return to my safe little home in Swansea. However, three more days remained. I prayed fervently that no one else would go missing or die.

Looking out the balcony doors, I could see that the ship was already docked at Road Town on the island of Tortola. We'd obviously made up time during the night.

The phone rang, breaking the peaceful silence. I quickly grabbed it and said, "Good morning."

"Good morning," Jane replied. "How are you guys doing?"

"We managed to sleep a little," I replied.

"Well, Rick and I have been talking, and we think there's a criminal on board who has targeted us for some reason. We may still be in danger. So we five should stay together from now on, at least as much as possible. We don't want anyone else to go missing."

"That's a good idea. Are you guys on your way to breakfast?"

"We just woke up ourselves. How about if we meet you in half an hour? Is that enough time?"

"I'm sure it'll be fine. I'll wake Melinda up now. See you then."

"Ta," Jane replied and hung up.

I shook Melinda's shoulder and she woke up quickly, slightly startled. "Bad news?" she mumbled as she sat up and stretched. It wasn't an unfair assumption.

"No. Jane just called. She and Rick think that there must be a criminal targeting our group, so we should all stay together from now on."

"I agree. Are they at breakfast already?"

"No. We're supposed to meet them in half an hour."

"Okay, I'm on board. You take the first shower while I try to wake up."

It was closer to forty minutes when Melinda and I appeared in the casual dining room.

We saw Jane and Rick in line for breakfast and waved a cheery hello. They smiled back.

"Did you talk to Sylvia this morning?" I asked them.

"We did, but she said she's not hungry," Jane answered

By the time we finally sat down, our good mood had fled. In those few minutes, memories had come flooding back of Phoebe, Duncan, and Liz.

"I can't eat," Jane said. "I have to find out if there's any news about Duncan's plane or what will happen with Liz's body. Stay here while I call Miss Carlisle."

Jane walked to a corner where shipboard only phones were available for everyone to use. She spoke for a few moments and then returned to us, where we were making half-hearted stabs at our breakfast.

"Well?" Rick asked.

"They found some wreckage of Duncan's plane, but no life raft and no survivors."

"Were they going to tell us?" I asked, peeved that one of us had had to call.

"Yes, when they thought we were all up."

"And Liz?" Melinda asked.

"Her sister will fly down and accompany the body back to the States. There's nothing we need to do."

"But we still don't know what happened to Phoebe," Melinda moaned. "Or how Liz got into the water."

"No," Rick said. "I guess we don't."

We ate in silence for a few moments. It occurred to me that we might never know what happened to Phoebe, but I kept this thought to myself.

"Rick and I talked again about going home," Jane finally said. "But we agreed that it would be too expensive, and it's not going to change anything that's happened. I'm sure the cruise line is not going to refund our money, so we might as well stay. After today we head back to New York anyway. We've got two full days at sea, so

I think I'd like to take an excursion today and try to get my mind off everything's that happened. Will you think me selfish and uncaring if I do?" She looked at all of us for affirmation with pleading eyes.

"I agree with Rick that we should stay together, and no, I don't think you're being selfish," Melinda responded. "Have you made any plans for Tortola?"

"We thought we'd do the excursion to Mount Sage National Park," Rick said. "Shall we all go?"

I hesitated to answer. I enjoyed hiking, but I wasn't sure I was up for the heat and humidity.

"It's not a lot of hiking or I wouldn't have signed up for it," Jane added, guessing why Melinda and I hesitated to answer. "And the trees will provide plenty of shade."

"But you're climbing a mountain," Melinda burst out, still unsure. I think she was more concerned for Jane than for herself.

"The brochure said the safari bus will take us most of the way up," Jane patiently explained, "and that a person need only be 'reasonably fit' to manage the walking. There are also benches to rest on. I think I can do it."

"What about Sylvia?" Melinda asked.

"We'll stop by her stateroom and ask her," Jane said. "You both in?"

I still hesitated, saying at last, "I'm fine with it."

Melinda grudgingly agreed.

"We meet in the auditorium at ten," Rick informed us, rising from the table. "See you then." He and Jane strolled away.

I said to Melinda, "I have a bad feeling about this."

"*You* do? I'm going to lose my breakfast. Let's get back to our stateroom."

Before we could leave, Elvis appeared, alert and grinning, with eyes only for Melinda.

After saying hello, he asked, "What are your plans for today?"

"We're taking the tour of Mount Sage," she said. "Want to join us?"

"No thanks. I'm allergic to everything green and growing. Meet me later tonight for a drink?"

"I'd love to," Melinda replied, with the biggest smile I'd yet to see this whole cruise.

With that Elvis ambled away, and Melinda squeezed my hand. "So far so good," she smiled.

We went back and put on long pants, long-sleeved shirts, socks, and sneakers. I'd had chiggers when I went to Girl Scout camp at age ten, and I didn't want to repeat the experience. I had to dig around for my hat and sunglasses, but was ready to head out with Melinda at 9:45 sharp.

When we got to the auditorium, there were forty or fifty passengers waiting to either sign up or confirm their reservations for the excursion. Sven, looking very tall and tan in khaki hiking shorts and a white golf shirt, was speaking to a small group about the beauties of Mount Sage.

When he saw Melinda and me, he excused himself and came over. Behind him, we saw Jane and Rick enter the back of the auditorium.

As he approached I said, "Hi, Sven. Is there room on the excursion for two more?"

"Of course," he replied. "I'll take care of it myself. I'm so glad you're joining us. Since you're here, you might as well enjoy this wonderful mountain. I'll be going along too, so I'll keep an eye on you." Then he winked at me and went back to the other group.

As we waited, I saw Alastair enter the auditorium and sit down. I didn't see Casandra. I was curious. Was he taking the excursion by himself? Was Casandra still angry with him? I'd probably never know, and in truth, it was none of my business.

Jane and Rick came down the aisle to us, and the first thing Melinda asked was "Where's Sylvia?"

"She said she's feeling ill and wants to stay in her stateroom today. I imagine its grief, or it might be the virus."

"I hope she's okay," Melinda said. "Maybe I should stay here and try to talk to her."

"I doubt she'll let you," Rick said. "She wouldn't answer the door when we knocked. Jane finally called and she pretty much said she wanted to be left alone."

"Well, okay. I'll go," Melinda said, but you could tell she was worried.

Promptly at ten, we were ushered out of the auditorium and toward the elevators. It seemed to me we spent half our time on board the ship either in the elevators or waiting for them, a good reason why I was starting to take the stairs when just going between one or two decks.

When we'd all assembled at deck four, we filed out of the ship, each of us stopping at the Security checkpoint to have our IDs scanned. Once on the pier, safari buses were waiting for us.

Sven directed us to ours.

Once everyone had boarded the buses, we began our trip through Road Town and up to Mount Sage National Park. On the way, our tour guide, a handsome young islander named Nico, told us the park was ninety-two acres of an amazing assortment of trees, bushes, and wildlife. Most of the park was 1000 feet above sea level, which included the peak at 1,716 feet. We soon arrived and disembarked in the car park where Nico urged us to look at the view. A stunning panorama of land, sea, and sky lay before us, starting from the sparkling sand beaches of the island, then westward for a view of Puerto Rico out across the aquamarine Caribbean, and then south to the Sir Francis Drake Channel.

I saw Alastair talking to two people I didn't recognize. I pointed him out to Melinda. "I wonder where Casandra is," I commented.

"Looks like trouble in paradise," she said. "I just hope he stays away from us."

We started out at a slow pace on the Main Trail. I was surprised at the slim girth of the amber-barked trees that populated either side of the dirt path. The leaves appeared high up on the trunks and provided much-needed shade, while filtering the sun's rays into myriad narrow shafts of light that gave a magical feel to the forest. I'd have to keep on the lookout for Oberon and Titania hiding amidst the golden beams and shadows. Would Puck perchance play a trick on us? I hoped not.

The first side trail we took led to the mahogany plantation. Nico informed us that these wide-branching trees were not native to the island and had been imported from South America. Some were now twenty years old and approaching their mature height of seventy feet or more. The wood was smooth and glistened in the moist air.

From here, we returned to the Main Trail and passed through a green-painted wooden gate and under a similarly green sign with yellow lettering that spelled out: "Welcome to Sage Mountain National Park Declared in 1964." Walking sticks were arranged near the gate, and Nico urged all of us of "mature age" to take one and return it at the end of our hike. Jane, Melinda, and I took one. Rick did not. I'm sure he felt that, since he was in such good shape, he didn't need it. Because the path itself was littered with leaves and small branches, I found the walking stick a real help in negotiating the foot-snatching roots hidden by dead leaves and debris — Puck's snares, no doubt.

Sven was shadowing Melinda and me and contributing small observations about the scenery. Jane and Rick lagged a bit behind the group and seemed to be enjoying their own company as much as the lush woods and shrubbery. Alastair was nowhere to be seen. Sven said we were nearing the highest point on the island, but because of the dense growth of trees and bushes, there was no view.

As we continued wandering along the Rainforest Trail, Sven pointed out the glossy leaves of coco plum shrubs, enormous elephant ear vines, and the amazing fern trees that had no bark or wood but seemed to spring Pan-like from just a cluster of leaves. He also pointed out the grand White Cedar, which he said was BVI's national tree.

Occasionally, a lizard would scamper across our path. Sven told us to be on the lookout for the gray turtle dove, the island's national bird. We never saw one, but we did hear their distinctive tur-tur call. No one spoke as we walked beneath the trees. Leaves and small sticks crunched beneath our feet; the air was filled with golden sun and the soft cooing of the doves. I stopped for a moment and looked up, allowing myself to feel inspired by this outdoor cathedral.

Enhancing the ethereal feel of the forest was the nearness of Sven who, as we'd been hiking along the path, had been guiding me with his hand cupped lightly under my left elbow. It wasn't an unpleasant touch.

After a while, we came to what were called simply The Steps, a steep wooden stairway with a rope handrail, leading down to a deep ravine. Nico announced that at the foot of the stairs was the best-preserved part of the forest. The steps looked rickety, damp, and slippery, not surprising given the rain forest climate. Our guide said he wouldn't recommend our climbing down, but he would wait for those who wanted to chance it. Jane and Rick caught up to us here. Jane said she didn't want to go down, but Rick said he would and carefully started down the steps, right hand clutching the rope.

Melinda said, "I'm game" and followed Rick. I looked at Sven. "What do you think?" I asked.

"I'll hold onto you," he assured me, and I started down, the four of us proceeding slowly and testing each step as we went.

Behind us, other members of the tour began their descent, but they weren't being as cautious as we were. I glanced behind us as the steps began to vibrate with the force of ten men and women in different rhythms hurrying down to the bottom. Suddenly, Alastair, with his cap on backward and arms akimbo, started to elbow past me. His jostling caused me to let go of the rope, and immediately, I began to fall. In a panic, I grabbed for Sven and clutched his arm, causing him to topple off the steps too. Falling, I sensed the emptiness of nothing beneath me and my stomach lurched with fear. Still holding on to Sven's arm, I watched him plummet down beside me.

As I fell, I heard people yelling, but I couldn't respond. I lost my grip on Sven and abruptly landed in a tangle of branches. The boughs held me in their prickly grasp as I caught my breath and realized I was not dead.

"You okay?" asked Sven, whose weight had propelled him deeper into the bush. I looked over and saw we were only a few feet from the ground. He seemed unhurt and easily set his feet on the ground and reached up for me. If I just turned to one side, the bush would depress enough to allow me to roll off. Holding Sven's hand, I was able to do just that, and I was soon standing up on solid ground.

"You sure you're alright?" he asked, worried.

"I think so."

"Any cuts or scratches?"

"My long sleeves and pants saved the day, but you seemed to have picked up a few."

I eyed the nasty lines of scarlet on both cheeks and running down his arms and calves.

"Had worse," he replied. "She's alright," Sven shouted up at the others. "It's okay, you can come down now. Just be careful."

Unnerved by my accident, I lost all interest in seeing the best-preserved part of the forest. Meanwhile, Sven had recovered and taken over as guide for the others. I looked around for Alastair, but didn't see him.

I headed back to the steps where Melinda and Rick were waiting for me.

"Are you sure you're okay?" Melinda asked.

"I'm sure. Just rattled a bit."

As the others milled around, Melinda and I started back up, Melinda leading the way.

As I climbed the first few steps, I felt my heart begin to pound like a fist trying to punch through my ribs. Taking another few

steps, I sensed panic rising in my throat and felt anxiety, like thick
rubber bands, encircling my chest. Sweat began pouring down my
forehead, almost blinding my vision. I had to pause to wipe it off
with my sleeve.

"I don't think I can move," I said shakily to Melinda, on the step
above me. "I'm scared to death."

"You'll be alright," she said calmly. "I'll help you. Just look at
my feet and nowhere else. Every time I pick up *my* right foot, you
put *your* right foot where mine was. When I lift up my left foot, you
put your left foot there. Don't look up or over, just concentrate on
my feet. Can you do that?"

"I think so."

"Okay, here we go."

I was trembling. I'm frightened of heights anyway, and now
I didn't think I could move. I had been alright when Sven was
behind me when I started down, but now, without him, I was in the
midst of a full-blown panic attack. The people at the bottom had
begun to ascend the steps behind me. Their presence only unnerved
me more. It was too late to turn around and go back.

"You can do it," Melinda softly urged me. "Just look at my feet
and your feet...nowhere else. You'll be okay."

She lifted up her right foot and put it on the next higher step.
I held my breath and put my right foot where hers had been, while
clutching the rope railing with both hands. I was now standing
shoulder to shoulder with Melinda on the narrow step. Slowly
she moved her left foot and placed it on the next higher step.
Carefully, I put my left foot where hers had been, and then I let my
breath out. I'd conquered one step.

We continued in this fashion, one step at a time, slowly picking
up speed as we went up the remaining steps. By the time we
reached the top I was covered in perspiration and breathing in
little puffs like a woman in labor. When we were finally on solid
ground, I don't know which relieved me more, the fact that I had
made it safely up the steps or that my fall had not resulted in any
broken bones.

"I'm sorry," Alastair apologized as he climbed into view. "I was
just in a hurry to get to the bottom. I had to find some place to pee."

"All's well that ends well," I said, but a small voice inside
wondered if he hadn't done it on purpose. I wasn't sure why he
would single me out, but I *had* been asking a lot of questions.

"That bloody Alastair always has to cause trouble," Melinda muttered to me.

Melinda's use of the local lingo made me smile.

"The tour's about over," Sven said as the last of the tourists came to the top. "When we get back to Road Town, we'll stop for food and drinks.

Our group slowly made their way back along the looping trail to the car park. When we took our seats on the safari bus, Alastair stopped at my seat and told me he'd buy me a drink at lunch.

"Thank you," I said. "I need one."

"You and me both," he said and went back to his seat.

CHAPTER SEVENTEEN
PUSSER'S PUB

Nico said we would be stopping at Pusser's Road Town Pub and Company Store. When we laughed at the funny name, he smiled and explained that "pusser" was Royal Navy slang for "purser," the one on a sailing vessel who was, at one time, responsible for giving seamen their daily ration of rum. We pulled up to a striking white building of three stories with a stark red roof. It overlooked the Road Town harbor and declared its name, Pusser's Co Store & Pub, in yellow paint on a large green sign. Nico told us not to be disturbed by the chickens running freely around the veranda.

We disembarked and walked through the porch, where folks were already dining, and into an air-conditioned Victorian bar that welcomed the hot and tired traveler with gleaming wood panels and cool air from swirling ceiling fans. Color was splashed everywhere, from the flags on the wall, to the orange life preservers hanging from the ceiling, to the stained glass windows and lamps.

Sven said he recommended ordering a Pusser's Painkiller which would arrive in its very own "take-home" white mug. This drink, a mixture of fruit juice and rum, could be ordered as a number one, two, or three, designating how much rum the bartender should provide.

Hot and sticky from our hike, Rick, Jane, Melinda, and I voted to sit indoors in the cool, dry air. Sven said he would be walking around and visiting all the ship's passengers in case they had any questions. He told us there was no reason to hurry to return to the bus if we wanted to rest here for a while; tour buses would be making trips back to the ship all afternoon. We all nodded our heads in gratitude.

A young, golden-skinned waitress handed round menus that featured jerk pork, jerk chicken, sirloin burgers, and pizza. I hadn't seen pizza at all on the cruise ship, so I ordered that and a number one Painkiller. Melinda was sharing my pizza, but chanced a number two Painkiller. Jane opted for a non-alcoholic ice tea, and Rick for an island-brewed beer.

No one brought up the names of those now missing from our group, and we enjoyed a wonderful respite from our worries. When our drinks arrived, we were surprised to see that the rum, which came in its own small glass, was black as tar.

We ate and drank as we recalled our hike through Mount Sage National Park—what our favorite views were and what it would be like to live here full-time. Jane said it would be a dream come true to have a little pink cottage with a large flower garden and a view of the ocean. Rick said it was too hot and humid for him, and he wondered which of his favorite TV channels he'd have to do without.

Alastair came by carrying another drink for me. I hadn't planned on inviting him to stay, but he sat down, anyway, in the chair I was saving for Sven.

"I'm truly sorry, Emily, that my clumsiness made you fall off the steps. I've been kind of weird since Phoebe disappeared, and now Casandra's mad at me, so I'm feeling out of sorts, and I really needed to pee back there."

Poor baby, I thought sarcastically, *you don't get any sympathy from me.* His explanation for his misbehavior had nothing to do with caring about Phoebe and everything to do with how it affected him.

"Do you guys know anything more than the other passengers about what happened to Phoebe?" he asked.

"No, nothing," Jane answered. "She disappeared, and the Security cams can't positively identify her as going overboard. We haven't found her or her body anywhere on the ship. Did you know that Duncan had to be medevacked to the mainland and his plane crashed in the ocean?"

"No! How awful! Bride and groom both gone. What a story! I noticed Sylvia and Liz aren't here either. Are they okay?"

We hesitated and looked at each other. Then Rick spoke up.

"Liz is dead. Her body was found by some men on a ship off the island of St. Kitts." He quickly added, "Sylvia isn't feeling well...not surprisingly."

Alastair looked shocked, but before he could respond, Sven arrived and pulled over a chair to join us. "How's everyone doing?" he asked.

We held up mugs and glasses—our second round of drinks. "We're fine," Rick said, speaking for all of us.

Alastair got up to leave, but Sven waved at him to sit down. "Why don't you stay, Alastair?"

Alastair looked doubtful but returned to his seat.

"Well, with you all in one spot," Sven began, "I'd like to tell you some of what we've found out about the night Mrs. Blumen disappeared. Passengers have come forward with some interesting stories about what happened that night, although no one saw Phoebe go overboard. What they have told us is that Phoebe, Sylvia, and Liz were drinking and joking around over by the railing of deck thirteen. More than one passenger said that Phoebe removed her diamond ring and handed it to Sylvia, who dropped it, and then the ring fell through the railing."

Jane spoke up quickly, "But neither Sylvia nor Liz ever told us this. Why would they lie?"

We all shook our heads in disbelief.

"Anything falling from deck thirteen would just wind up on deck twelve, right?" I said.

"We think somebody on deck twelve picked it up," Sven said and turned his gaze to Alastair.

"Why are looking at me?" he demanded. "I was just standing on deck twelve, enjoying the breeze, and out of nowhere, a diamond ring lands at my feet. Of course I picked it up! I had no way of knowing it was Phoebe's."

"You didn't hear them talking just one deck above you?" Jane asked.

"No, I didn't. I mean, I heard women talking, but I didn't know who they were."

"You didn't recognize your ex-wife's voice?" Jane was astonished.

"No, the band was playing. It was hard to hear."

"And you didn't think to take it to Security in case someone was looking for it?" I asked. Sven and I locked eyes.

"Why would I do that? Someone had obviously thrown it away," he answered.

"Or maybe they just dropped it," I responded.

"Finders keepers," Alastair said with a self-righteous glare aimed at me.

"Likely story," Jane sneered. "You've known us since high school. You'd recognize the voices."

"Maybe I was a little drunk and feeling a little sick. All I did was pick something up off the ground. That's not a crime."

"But you didn't report it to Security," Sven interrupted. "I'm sure you knew it was an expensive piece of jewelry and that the owner would be looking for it."

"No, I didn't know that," he continued in his absurd attempt to justify the theft. I don't think any of us believed him.

"What happens now?" asked Rick.

"Nothing until we get back to New York. Then we'll turn it over to the FBI."

"The FBI?" Jane said, concerned.

"Yes, that's who has jurisdiction for most crimes at sea involving US citizens."

"Will I be arrested?" Alastair asked.

"No, we're not pressing charges...unless, of course, something else comes to light. We will, however, need the ring."

"Casandra can't get it off her finger," Alastair said. "We'll have to see a jeweler in New York and have it removed."

"Why don't you take Casandra to the infirmary and see if someone there can remove it?" Sven said. "If not, I'm sure the FBI will have a suggestion."

"I'm a dead man," Alastair said, shaking his head. We all glared at him for the inappropriateness of the comment. He didn't seem to notice.

"There's a tour bus heading back to the ship now," Sven said. "We should all take it. It's almost four o'clock, and the ship leaves at five."

Slowly we finished our drinks and hoisted ourselves from our seats. This day had been perhaps the most stunningly beautiful and most disturbing day of our whole trip so far. We didn't speak much as we settled our tab with the waitress and made our way out to the parking lot and climbed aboard the bus.

Glancing at the sky, I noticed clumps of dark clouds amassing on the western horizon. I hoped we'd reach the ship before the rain began.

Sitting in one of the bus seats was Ariana Muller. The other band members had taken seats behind her. I decided to take the empty seat next to her.

"You don't look very happy," she remarked. "It was a beautiful mountain, *ja*?"

"Yes."

"But you've had some bad news from the cruise director?"

"I'm afraid so."

"We will play something happy in the auditorium tonight."

"I'm not sure if that will help, but I appreciate the gesture."

"Next cruise will be better."

"I don't think there'll be a next one."

"Sure, not all cruises have bad things happen. Now the bad things are out of the way. You can only have happy cruises."

"If you say so."

We sat in silence until the bus reached the dock. Hurrying against the wind and the threatening weather, we reboarded the ship.

"See you tonight," Ariana said as she disappeared into an elevator.

"Yes," I said and turned to look for Melinda.

"Bad news," she whispered to me. "Tell you when we get to our stateroom."

Rick, Jane, Alastair, Melinda, and I stood back while the German members took up all the elevators. We waited patiently for the cars to return. No one felt like talking. I looked for Sven and noticed he had gone.

Back in our stateroom, Melinda shut the door and said, "Alastair took me aside earlier and asked if he and Casandra could join us at our table for dinner. He said his table was mostly young couples with children, and since we now have empty chairs, would he mind if they joined us. Empty chairs! What nerve! But I didn't know how to say no."

"Could be interesting," I replied. "I'm guessing Alastair has to tell Casandra where her ring came from before she hears it from one of us."

"Well, just in case he hasn't told her, let's try to work it into the conversation."

"You're bad!"

"I'm good bad, but not evil," she joked.

"No, I think tonight you might just be evil."

At that moment the ship lurched, and we ran to our balcony to say good-bye to the islanders waving at us from Tortola. The rain had begun, and in the gentle shower, I suddenly realized we hadn't spent any time on our balcony during the cruise. Despite the rain, the air was softly warm and fragrant with the lush scents of tropical trees and flowers. Smiling at Melinda, I suggested that this was a good time to appreciate our balcony. We settled into the chairs, sheltered from the rain by the balcony above us; put our feet up on the railing; and enjoyed the sound of the rain and the aromatic breeze. For just a moment, the clouds in the west lifted, and we glimpsed the late afternoon sun, serene and breathtakingly beautiful as its golden rays highlighted the purple undersides of the clouds and lit up the lush green of the mountains. Maybe I *could* come back someday.

CHAPTER EIGHTEEN
THE PILL BOTTLE

Dinner was casual that evening, which on a cruise ship means not shorts or jeans but business casual slacks with sport coats for men and dresses or skirts for women. Rick was nautical in a navy blazer and white pants; Jane was regal in a gold pants suit. The events on the cruise seemed to have drawn them closer together. After the séance's revelations and ensuing argument, they appeared to have made peace and were enjoying a second honeymoon, or at least, as much as one could, given the loss of three of our party.

Alastair arrived in a brown plaid jacket paired with the ubiquitous khakis, and Casandra was resplendent in an oatmeal-colored sweater dress that stopped just inches below her panties. She wore a thick gold necklace with a large turquoise stone in the shape of a quarter moon. It lay nestled between her breasts like a small animal that had found a soft home.

Melinda had dug out a scarlet peasant skirt-and-blouse set that looked like something that belonged in the German band wardrobe. Fashion was not always her strong suit. I wore my go-with-everything black skirt and a lilac silk shell.

Sylvia didn't make an appearance in the dining room.

"She's still ill," Jane said. It then occurred to me that we hadn't seen Sylvia the whole day. We only had Jane and Rick's assurance that she was in her stateroom. Were they hiding something? Would we find out that Sylvia was missing too? I'd have to find a way to check on her.

Alastair was still feeling badly about causing my fall, so he ordered a bottle of champagne from the wine steward who, shortly thereafter, presented a bottle for Alastair's approval. I felt a little guilty drinking a celebratory beverage, but decided not to rain on Alastair's parade. The champagne would be a delicious complement to the crab bisque soup and spinach salad that I'd ordered.

It was steak night, and we were told we could have seconds, but we would need to tell our waiter when he took our order how many steaks we would need. Jane, Melinda, and I were content with one, but Rick and Alastair each ordered two. Casandra informed us all that she didn't eat the meat of her own species and got the salmon. No one in our group raised an eyebrow.

We exchanged awkward smiles for about five minutes, and then Melinda innocently asked Casandra to show us her ring. Casandra's face contorted with a look of confusion, and she turned to Alastair. He understood her and gave her a wry smile, which told us that she knew where the ring had come from. Then he nodded toward the rest of us. His gesture clearly said "Show them."

Casandra held out her left hand, and we all gawked at the beautiful ring, but said nothing.

"I know it was Phoebe's," Casandra began. "Alastair told me. And you all can have it back as soon as I get the damned thing off my finger."

"What would we do with it?" Jane asked. "Phoebe and Duncan are gone."

"You could give it to Phoebe's daughter," Casandra suggested. "I certainly don't want it. I'm not wearing another woman's engagement ring."

"She's Alastair's daughter too," Melinda pointed out.

"Right," said Casandra, "I'm an idiot."

No one spoke up to disagree.

Melinda asked, "Alastair, are you sure you didn't see anything else that night on deck twelve?"

"No, I'm sorry, but I didn't. I know I was a coward. The minute that ring hit the deck I grabbed it and ran. I didn't want to know who it belonged to. All I could think about was how much money it would save me."

Alastair looked truly contrite. His brown eyes were downcast, and his mouth was shaped in a sad frown, one more set of lines in a worn, middle-aged visage. He'd obviously acted on impulse, and who among us hadn't done that on occasion. However, it was still a theft, and he was responsible for the consequences.

The wine steward returned with the champagne on a tray with six fluted glasses.

"To happy endings," Alastair toasted, lifting his glass high.

As a group, we seemed to agree to ignore the unsuitability of this remark and raised our glasses likewise.

"To the continued good health of those present," Melinda sweetly suggested, as we sampled the champagne.

"Thank you, Melinda," Jane said.

Now that we'd humored Alastair, it was back down to the business of Phoebe's disappearance. We patiently waited while Dmitri served our soup, holding our tongues until he walked away.

Then, as if reading our minds, Casandra asked, "Could Alastair's stealing this ring have had anything to do with his first wife's disappearance? Couldn't Duncan have been murderously angry at Phoebe because she lost it?"

"We don't know," Melinda replied. "The two things did happen on the same night. However, another scenario might be that Alastair lay in wait for Phoebe to come down to retrieve the ring and pushed her overboard."

Alastair's head reared up from his soup.

"You wouldn't have had to pay alimony with Phoebe gone," I stated.

Alastair stared at us in utter confusion.

"My goodness, Alastair, you wouldn't actually do something like that?" Casandra said, visibly shocked at this thought.

"Of c-c-course not," he stuttered, taking a quick gulp of champagne. "That would be murder. Do you really think I'm a murderer?"

"Of course not," Casandra said thoughtfully, twirling her champagne glass and staring at the bubbles rising from the bottom. "But I might want to delay the wedding until we have some more information about Phoebe."

"We might never know what happened to her," Jane said.

"Well, I would like to wait and see," Casandra replied.

"I think you're being smart," I smiled at her. Casandra had just risen ten points in my estimation.

"Okay...okay, but I'm very offended that you think I could do something like that," Alastair interjected.

"We'll talk about it later," Casandra said. "I have another mystery to ask about since you're all here. I found this on our balcony the first evening of our cruise."

She pulled from her purse an amber pill bottle and held it up for us all to see. "The name has been ripped off, but I recognize the pills inside. It's a diuretic called furosemide, and it's used for congestive heart disease. My father takes it. Do you all have any idea whose it is, and how it got onto our balcony?"

We were stunned into silence. It might be Duncan's missing pill bottle. Was this Alastair's work also? Was he so jealous of Phoebe that he would try and kill her husband by hiding his medication? But that made no sense because with Duncan gone, Phoebe would need that alimony.

We all quickly glanced at each other.

"That might be Duncan's," I replied. "He said he was sure he had packed it, and afterward, it went missing. Did someone take it?" I looked around the table at everyone.

"Don't look at me," Alastair said. "What possible reason would I have to harm Duncan?"

"Don't look at me or Rick," Jane declared. "We loved them both."

"Sylvia or Liz?" I asked.

"But how would it get onto our balcony?" Casandra asked.

"What's your stateroom number?" I asked her.

"7103," she said.

"That's directly below Liz and Sylvia's stateroom," Melinda pointed out. "They could have easily leaned out theirs and thrown it onto yours."

"They were probably aiming for the ocean but missed," I said.

"But why?" Casandra asked.

"I don't know."

"I can't believe it," Jane shook her head in disbelief. "We've known Sylvia and Liz for years and years. Is this some weird expression of jealousy?"

"Or psychosis?" Casandra suggested.

Once again, my opinion of Casandra shot up.

Our steaks had been sitting untouched before us. We all seemed to decide unconsciously that we would think better with full stomachs and began to address our meal. Knives and forks scrapped the china as we ate and thought, chewing both physically and metaphorically on the problem before us.

When we were about halfway through our meal, Dmitri appeared pushing a pastry cart of chocolate concoctions and cheesecake.

"Dessert?" he asked.

"No," we all said and shook our heads. It seemed too cruel to enjoy dessert as we discussed the deaths of our friends.

"I'd like to talk to Sylvia without the rest of you," I said, having thought of a plan to check on her. "Maybe, since I'm a disinterested third party, she'll be more honest with me. And she knows me from the bank. What do you think?"

"It certainly wouldn't hurt," Melinda acknowledged.

What I didn't tell them was that I was going to find Sven and ask him to accompany me. I still considered him a suspect too. I had questions for both him and Sylvia.

With a confident "I'll see you later," I left my seat and walked toward the exit. I spotted Dmitri as I neared the doorway and asked him, "Did any of your friends change their mind about helping us?"

"No, sorry. They have not."

"Thank you anyway," I shrugged and exited the dining room. I took the stairs down two flights to deck nine to look in the auditorium to see if Sven was there preparing for tonight's show.

I found him backstage, fiddling with the lights.

"Hi," I said. "I want to ask a favor."

He turned around quickly and gave me a grin.

"Anything for a lovely lady."

He wore a dark suit with a white shirt and turquoise tie. With his tan face and sparkling eyes, he looked quite handsome.

"I'd like to talk to Sylvia with you present. Are you free right now?"

"No problem. I have an hour before the show."

CHAPTER NINETEEN

Deck Twelve

Sven led the way, and we walked companionably out of the theatre.

"Are you all recovered from this morning?" he asked.

"I'm fine. How about you? I don't see any scratches."

"I put some makeup over them, but don't tell anyone," he said with a conspirator's whisper.

I looked closely at his face. If you were next to him, you could just barely make out the concealer dotted on spots across his forehead and both cheeks.

"It's almost impossible to tell. You must have practice at applying it."

"I've fallen into more bushes than I care to admit."

"I'm sure you've got a good story or two about that."

"Another time. Let's take the stairs." We quickly walked down to deck eight, turned left, and made our way down the hallway to the door of 8103. Sven tapped lightly on Sylvia's door.

Sylvia called out, "Come in."

Sven opened the door, and I saw Sylvia sitting at the desk with a crossword puzzle spread out before her. At least she wasn't missing.

"I'm sure Liz won't mind that I'm doing her puzzles," she said.

"I wondered if you'd be okay talking to me a bit about Liz," I said. "Feel like a walk around the deck?"

"Is he coming?" she asked, nodding at Sven.

"I brought him along for protection," I joked.

Sylvia took it seriously. "Against *me*?"

"No, of course not. I'm kidding. I thought you'd enjoy his company."

Sven raised questioning eyebrows at me. I ignored him.

Sylvia said, "Okay." She got up to join us.

"You can hold my hand," she said to Sven.

"That won't be necessary," he replied. "I'll just walk behind the two of you."

We left the stateroom in silence and walked to the elevators.

"Which deck?" Sven asked.

"Deck twelve," I said quickly. Not only was it partially sheltered from the rain, I wanted to return to the probable scene of the crime.

For once, an empty car came as soon as we pressed the Up button.

On deck twelve, we made our way through the heavy glass doors and out onto the deck. A retractable glass dome had been extended over the pool area to allow passengers to use it even in the rain. I was surprised at all the families still at the pool at this late hour. We could hear squealing and giggling — lots of distraction.

"Let's walk around toward the back of the ship," Sven suggested.

When we got to the quieter area, we continued walking. The rain had stopped, at least temporarily, but a light fog was filling in the gaps between us.

"Shouldn't people be asked to leave the pool?" I said to Sven. "You could lose someone in this fog, especially a child."

"I'm sure they'll sound the bell for everyone to get out any moment now," he replied.

I turned to Sylvia, "Alastair told us about Phoebe's engagement ring going over the side of deck thirteen. The Security cameras show you being there with Phoebe and Liz. Why didn't you tell us?"

"I don't know," she said, suddenly uncooperative.

"Did you know that Alastair picked the ring up?"

"No, but that explains why we couldn't find it."

"Can you tell me everything that happened that night?"

"Why should I tell you?"

"Why not? It might help us solve the mystery of Phoebe's disappearance. It always helps to keep reviewing the facts in hopes of finding a connection we didn't see before."

We rounded a corner and walked into a dense fog bank. The world became muffled in gray mist. I could no longer see the walls and railings and could barely make out my companions; only the soles of my feet connected me to the solid reality of the ship. While my senses were sorting out their new surroundings, we were suddenly startled by a loud "Brring! Brring!" echoing in the damp air. I guessed it was the bell that signaled for the pool to be emptied. On its heels came the deep-throated "Bong! Bong!" of the ship's fog horn, rattling my composure.

"Help!" suddenly broke through the background noise, and we all turned in the direction of the pool.

"I can't find my baby!" we heard a woman shriek, and Sven sprinted off to the rescue.

"We can continue without him," Sylvia said to me from seemingly nowhere. I resumed my steps, ears straining to catch her voice. As I walked, I entered deeper into the fog. I lost all sense of direction and trusted to Sylvia's voice to keep me close to her. The mist's sudden dampness gave me a chill, and I couldn't stop a shiver.

"What were we talking about?" Sylvia asked.

"I know you've had a difficult time of it these last few years," I began, redirecting our conversation. "It can't have been easy recovering from the loss of your husband. Especially with Phoebe and Duncan flaunting their relationship in your face."

Sylvia said nothing, so I returned to my first line of questioning.

"I was hoping you'd tell me more about what happened the night Phoebe disappeared. I'm trying to understand what might have happened. Maybe Duncan came looking for her. Maybe they argued. He wouldn't be happy about her losing the ring. Have you remembered anything more?"

"You're right," she said. "It's been very hard. Duncan should have married me instead of Phoebe. And he would have if she hadn't flirted with him right under my nose and lured him away."

I slowed my steps, hoping Sylvia would do the same. We were getting out of earshot of the pool. I shivered again with the cool wetness of the air on my arms. My stomach turned queasy as the unseen deck rose and fell beneath my feet.

Sylvia continued, "Well...that night, Liz and I decided to go to the midnight buffet...which we did...and afterward we decided to go up to the party deck and dance. When we got there, we saw Phoebe on the outside deck, sitting at a table having a drink by herself."

"What time was this?" I asked.

"I don't know, maybe twelve or twelve fifteen. Liz and I went out and sat down with her. Later, we all decided to go inside and dance. After a few songs we were tired and went outside again."

I could sense that Sylvia had stopped walking, so I stopped also.

"Phoebe was being her usual snotty self and showing off. She was holding out her hand so we could all admire her ring and how it sparkled in the moonlight. I asked her if I could try it on to see how it would look on me. She took it off and handed it to me." Sylvia paused, then went on, "I tried putting it on my ring finger, but it didn't fit. It made me mad, even Phoebe's fingers were better than mine, slimmer and prettier.

"Just to mess with her, I faked tossing it over the railing. You should have seen the look on her face! I loved it. Such panic!" Sylvia made an odd sound—half wheeze, half chuckle—an eerie sound.

"Then," she continued, "I dropped it. I was horrified, really, as I watched it bounce under the railing and over the side. I knew, though, that it probably just landed on deck twelve below."

"How did Phoebe react?"

"She got all hysterical." Sylvia coughed. "But I told her we'd just go down and pick it up. I shouted down to see if anyone was down there, but there was no reply. The band was pretty loud. There was a metal stairway right by where we were standing, and we all rushed down. However, when we got to the bottom, the ring wasn't there."

"That was a pretty nasty trick to pull," I commented. "What was Phoebe's reaction when you got down to deck twelve and the ring was gone?"

"She had quite the hissy fit, even though we were all frantically searching the deck on our hands and knees. When we couldn't find it, she started to cry. I asked her if the ring was insured, and the idiot told me they hadn't gotten around to doing that yet. So we started searching that much harder. After a few minutes, Liz and I were tired, so we suggested we stop looking and report it to Security in the morning. Phoebe wanted to keep looking, so Liz and I left her there. That's the truth. I don't know what happened after..."

I no longer heard Sylvia's voice in the deepening fog. I felt another panic attack starting as my heart began to beat more rapidly. My stomach quivered as if I might be ill, so I reached out, feeling for a railing or a wall to steady myself. Then, out of nowhere, I felt a hand grab me underneath my right knee and then another hand wrap around my right calf. There was a loud grunt, and before I could react, my right leg was lifted up and over the outside railing. Its cold metal felt slick and ominous. Although I was only a few pounds lighter than her, Sylvia was able to lift my whole right leg, leveraging my lower body along with it, up and over the railing. I was so surprised, I couldn't think.

I shouted "Hey!" and grabbed hold of the railing with both hands. I wrapped my arms around it, grasping for purchase on its wet and slippery surface. I could hear Sylvia panting with the effort to support me.

Trying to save myself, I took my left leg and threw it around the railing so that when she shoved me over the top I was clinging to it with my arms and legs wrapped around the thin metal tube, like a monkey hanging horizontally on a pole, except that I was hanging over the deep and deadly Atlantic Ocean.

My fear of heights went into overdrive. I could hear the engines churning away below and feel the spray of the ocean as the ship cut through the waves. I was going to die.

Sylvia struggled to untangle my legs, but I was just strong enough to make it difficult. It only took seconds, though, for my muscles to start aching from the strain of supporting me.

"You bitch..." she said to me, snorting, wheezing, and pulling frantically at my feet. "Let go, damn it, just let go..."

As my arms began screeching with pain and Sylvia was beginning to have some luck with pulling one leg away from the other, she suddenly let go of me.

Then Sven's face appeared almost on top of mine, his voice saying "It's okay. I've got you."

He put his arms around my shoulders and waist and lifted me back through the wide space between the two rungs of the railing. Next he laid me on the deck and helped me untangle myself.

"You bastard," Sylvia shouted at him. "You've ruined everything!"

The fog began to lift enough for me to see around me, and I watched Sven take off his tie, pull Sylvia's arms behind her back, and bind her wrists together.

I looked up at her from where I still lay, recovering, and asked, "Did you kill Phoebe?"

"Of course, you ninny," Sylvia replied, proud of it.

"You pushed her overboard?"

"She was light as a feather."

"How could you do such a thing?"

"You'd be surprised how easy it really is," she said with a crazed smile. "Once you flick on that little switch in your brain that says 'I can do this,' it happens so fast you don't even realize you've done it."

"And Liz?" I asked her. "Why did you kill Liz?"

"Because she killed Duncan," she replied and paused. The switch she spoke of in her brain must have flicked off because suddenly Sylvia started to cry, huge sobs that she tried to hide by lowering her head onto her chest. Her shoulders shook as she cried, "I was going to marry him once Phoebe was out of the way."

Sven took hold of one of her arms and with his other hand helped me to my feet. Together we turned back toward the center of the ship.

"Tell us about Duncan. Did you take his pills?" I said as we walked to the elevators.

"Liz did," Sylvia replied. "She took Duncan's pills out of Phoebe's bag when Phoebe left it on the table to go up to the lunch buffet on the first day.

"But why would Liz do that?"

"She hated him. She wanted to see him suffer. Said he'd blocked a promotion for her at work, because she wouldn't go out on a second date with him. But she didn't tell me about it until he was already in the infirmary, when it was too late for me to stop her."

"Did she want to kill him?"

"No, just punish him. But I didn't care about her stupid promotion. If his plane hadn't gone down, there might still have been a chance for me." Her face twisted into a self-pitying grimace as she spat out the next words. "I couldn't forgive her."

"And the note in Phoebe and Duncan's bedroom?"

"Did you like the poem? I wrote that. I got the porter to let me in before Phoebe and Duncan arrived. I wanted to ruin their honeymoon. I wanted Phoebe to feel insecure. I wanted to put a chink in that self-satisfied armor of hers. She was always saying how lucky she was. Well, she's not feeling lucky now."

"So...you didn't know Liz planned all along to harm Duncan."

"No."

"And when Duncan died, you blamed Liz?"

"Of course."

"How did you manage to kill Liz?"

"After we got the news about Duncan, I told her I needed a drink and asked her to go to the party deck with me. Then I got her to stop on deck twelve first so I could get a snack from the midnight buffet. When we got off the elevator, I suggested we take a minute to look at the moon from the promenade deck, and that's when I accused her of taking Duncan's pills. At first, she didn't admit to taking them, but after arguing with her that she was the only one who knew which pills were for what, she admitted it. I was so mad I acted before I even thought about it. She was as light as a child to pick up and lift over the railing. Just like Phoebe had been. Because of Liz, Duncan was dead. She deserved to die."

Liz and Sylvia amazed me. Who were they? And how had they lived such seemingly blameless lives so far only to commit these horrendous crimes now? Did the cruise transport them not only out of their physical home but their moral universe as well?

When we were back at Sylvia's stateroom, Sven opened the door and we went in.

"There'll be no more walks on deck," he said to her. "You're confined to your stateroom until we reach port. I'll be back in the morning. I'll send someone from Security to guard your door now, and someone else to take your statement." With nothing more to say, he and I left.

"Thank you," I said as we headed down the corridor to the opposite end of the ship where my room was. "I always seem to be thanking you. I wish I could buy you a drink. Would you like one of your non-alcoholic beers?"

"I would," he said.

We rode the elevators back up to the Old English pub, where Sven used the phone to request a Security detail for Sylvia. Then he ordered N.A. beer for him and a vodka and tonic for me. We took our drinks outside and sat on the deck. The rain and the fog were clearing up now. The clouds were moving aside to reveal a million twinkling stars in the midnight sky.

We didn't speak for a while. I was grateful for the warm night air and just being alive. I don't know what Sven's thoughts were. I imagined he was putting it all together in his mind for his report to the authorities.

"I hope it's over now," I said after several minutes. "I'm glad Sylvia is finally telling the truth. I'm feeling rather numb with the shock of it all."

Sven said, "Stay with me tonight." He draped his arm around my shoulders. "I'll make you forget about all this for a while. I'll be your refuge from the storm and your knight in shining armor."

"What a mix of metaphors," I teased. "So your interest in Sylvia was not sincere? I saw you guys Friday night walking with your arms around each other."

"She was a suspect early on. I was keeping tabs on her and trying to win her confidence."

"And me?"

He didn't answer. He just kissed me, and I have to admit, he stirred up feelings that made his offer more than tempting, almost a biological imperative. I resisted, though, and pushed him gently away, my hands softly massaging his shoulders even as I repelled him.

"This is not for me," I said. "I was never good at one-night stands. I become emotionally involved."

To his credit, he didn't pressure me.

"Let me walk you back to your stateroom, at least," he said. "It's my job to make sure you're safe. I almost flubbed it up there on deck twelve."

"Oh, that's right. The baby in the pool...were you able to save it?"

"Someone else had already pulled her up from the bottom. I just stuck around long enough to make sure she was breathing."

"You didn't save the baby, but you did save me. Do these acts of heroism happen on all your cruises?"

"No, this one is special."

I drank off the last of the vodka and tonic and rose to leave. Sven took one last sip of his beer and held my hand as we walked back to the elevators. We didn't speak as we rode down and continued our silence to my stateroom. At the door, I kissed him lightly.

"I need to say thank you one more time. I'm pathological that way."

"I was just doing my job, ma'am," he said with a short, mocking bow. "Take care, and see you tomorrow."

"Yes, tomorrow."

I opened the door and gave Sven a sad smile as I closed it.

"Was that Sven with you?" Melinda asked, looking up from her book.

"Yes."

"I applaud your self-restraint," she joked.

"I think he's been playing me because I might be a suspect, which is what he says he was doing with Sylvia. Whatever the reason, I'm probably a fool for missing out on what I'm sure would have been a night of blissful pleasure. Now, I have much more important news for you."

Calmly, I told her about Sylvia's confession that she'd pushed both Phoebe and Liz overboard, her attempt to kill me, Sven's rescue, and that Liz had stolen Duncan's pills and thrown them away.

Melinda listened in silence, her eyes wide with surprise.

"Em, you're so lucky Sven was there! How did you guess it was Sylvia? Did you plan that walk in order to trick Sylvia into revealing herself?"

"I wasn't sure it was Sylvia, but yes, I hoped she would. Or if it was Sven, maybe he would try something once he had Sylvia and me alone. For once in my life, I'm grateful that I'm not a tiny wisp of a person who could have easily been thrown overboard."

"I'm shocked that Liz and Sylvia could be so evil," Melinda said. "Who'd have thought two women who are my personal friends could be so hateful."

"Didn't you suspect either of them?"

"Sylvia, yes. I could feel all her ill will and her desperation. But Liz surprised me. I'm amazed at how well she hid her feelings from me."

I sighed. "I guess we just finish our cruise while Sylvia's under house arrest. The captain will probably turn her over to the authorities when we get back to New York. You know, I'm not tired at all; I need to unwind. Maybe I'll go listen to the German band."

"Do you mind going alone? I'm too tired."

"Oh, how was your date with Elvis?"

"Wonderful. That's all I'm saying right now."

"I understand. See you in half an hour."

"I'll probably be asleep."

"I won't be far behind."

On deck twelve, I decided to check out the selection of goodies in the midnight buffet. Choosing a bowl of fresh fruit, I took my snack to an empty table in the shadows where I could hear the band finish up their set with a rousing rendition of "Good Night Ladies."

When they were done, I saw Ariana place her trombone in a black carrying case and hand it to a tall man whose features I couldn't quite make out.

As they headed inside, the man grabbed Ariana's hand and pulled her close. They stopped briefly and enjoyed a long, passionate kiss. Ariana's free arm went up and around his neck, and his arm encircled her waist and pulled her close. After five seconds, he released her, took her hand, and they resumed their walk.

As they stopped beneath the light shining down on the doorway, I saw that the man was Sven.

Better her than me I thought and went back to my fruit.

FINAL DAYS

CHAPTER TWENTY

Going Home

When I awoke the next morning, I didn't want to get out of bed. All Mondays are a letdown, especially at the end of a vacation. These last two days would be spent at sea on our way back to New York, so there were no excursions to anticipate, no tropical islands to visit, no beaches on which to lay and enjoy the Caribbean sun. There was a much advertised Art Auction to be held Tuesday afternoon, but I had no interest in it.

The remnants of the Wayward Sisters, along with Rick and me, whiled away the next two days eating, reading, drinking, and gambling at the casino. Melinda and I didn't see Alastair or Casandra again.

Monday afternoon, Melinda asked if I minded if she spent the night with Elvis.

I said, "Of course not" and told her I was thankful she had warned me ahead of time. If I'd woken to find her missing, too, I'd have panicked big time.

However, the bad news was not over. Tuesday afternoon, the bar bill arrived.

"How did I drink four hundred dollars' worth of alcohol?" I screeched when I looked at the numbers in the little box at the bottom.

"Think about it," Melinda laughed. "Divide four hundred dollars by ten days and you get forty dollars a day. At roughly seven dollars a drink with another dollar for the tip, now you have eight dollars. That's only five drinks a day."

"*Only* five drinks a day? Did I really drink that much?"

"One or two in the afternoon, one before dinner, one with dinner, and two in the evening. That's nothing."

"Nothing? I'm going to abstain for the next month and let my system dry out."

"Sure, that's what they all say," Melinda said and threw her book on the floor. "Let's get ready for dinner."

As we sat in the formal dining room for the last time, Sven stopped by our table.

"What happens to Sylvia?" I asked.

"The authorities will be waiting for her in New York," Sven said. "I'll give them the security tapes and the blonde hairs for testing."

"Do people get arrested very often on cruise ships?" Melinda asked.

"Not as often as they could. Most of our problems are people drinking too much and men fighting. If nothing serious occurs, we won't file any charges, and when we dock, they'll walk off the ship without suffering any consequences."

"Pretty nice of you," I said.

"We don't want the bad publicity," Sven smiled.

"I guess we'll never find Phoebe's body now, will we?"

"Probably not," Sven mused.

"It's a big ocean," Melinda offered softly.

When I awoke early on Wednesday morning, I thought about Sylvia. I felt that I understood her all too well, except for the part where she actually murdered two people. As angry as women might get over some men's preference for eye candy over intelligence and good humor, women are equally at fault. We endure fools, abusers, and bums lazier than winter molasses just to have a man to come home to at night. Good or bad, he stands as our buffer against all the unknowns of the world and, most especially, against the black hole of loneliness.

I thought about Liz, so brave in her contempt for all men, then I corrected myself. No, she hadn't been brave; she'd been broken and hurting, emotionally curled up in a corner and licking her wounds, scratching at anyone that would come too close. What was the hope for the Liz's of this world? Certainly not the likes of Alastair or Sven.

I understood that Sven had only been interested in me as a conquest, but some part of me had responded to him. I realized, to my shame, that I was attracted to Sven just for the simple joy of the conquest, not to mention the assurance that I was still attractive. I was as foolish as anyone else, male or female.

The gentle rocking of the ship halted, and I felt the ship shudder as she bumped into her berth in New York City harbor. My first cruise was over. I felt much older than the woman who stood on the deck and waved good-bye to the Statue of Liberty; I felt I'd been away not ten days but ten years.

I was so looking forward to my solitary little cottage, my comfy old sofa, my lonely bed, and please, no ghosts.

THE END

Questions for the Author

How did you do your research? Have you been on many cruises?

Between 2003 and 2010, I enjoyed six marvelous cruises to Bermuda, the Eastern and Western Caribbean, and a tour of the Mediterranean. As far as I know, no one ever went missing on those vacations.

What inspired you to set a murder mystery on a cruise ship?

Two reasons. The first is the unsolved disappearance of George Smith IV, a bridegroom on his honeymoon who went missing from a cruise ship in the Aegean Sea on July 5, 2005.

In January of 2015, the Connecticut FBI closed its investigation, saying there was not enough evidence to prove that he had been murdered and ruled that his death was probably an accident.

My other reason was that a cruise ship is the perfect setting for a "cozy" mystery, where you have a confined space and limited number of suspects.

Do people go overboard that often?

According to CruiseJunkie.com (as reported in the Huffpost travel blog on 3/02/2015), there have been 243 cases of "man overboard" since 1995.

What are the chances for survival?

It depends on many factors: if they're seen going overboard, how far the person falls, and the temperature of the water. Upon hitting the water, limbs may be broken which could make it difficult to swim. The air can also be knocked out of you. If that happens, chances are you will automatically gasp for more air, and this may cause you to swallow water and subsequently drown.

If the water is cold, hypothermia can set in. It's recommended that a person not thrash about as this uses up valuable energy. Your best chance for survival is to remain positive and hope that you are seen and rescued. If the water is warm, such as in the Caribbean, you may be able to float for many hours before being noticed and rescued.

That being said, Cruise Line International reported that of the 96 people recorded as going overboard from 2009-2013, only twenty were rescued (as published by G.P. Wild (International) Limited December 2014).

Coming in 2018

Death on the Brandywine

A new Emily Menotti Mystery

Follow the clues with Emily Menotti as she unravels still more mysteries:

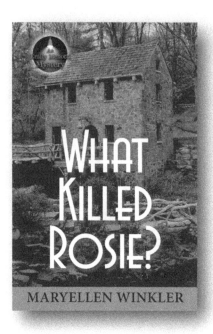

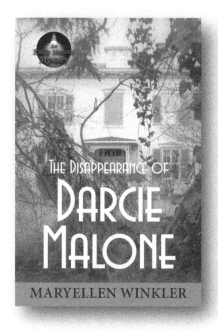

Who did Emily see in the laundromat doorway that warm May evening?

It looked like her old friend Rosie. Problem is, Rosie died of a heart attack five years ago, and now Rosie's old boyfriend is reporting strange occurrences at his condo. Is it Rosie's ghost demanding revenge? Or is someone trying to perpetuate a hoax? Join Emily as she searches among Rosie's acquaintances to find out what really killed Rosie.

On a warm September night in 1969, a young couple embarks on a romantic midnight picnic on the grounds of a legendary haunted house. By morning, the girl has disappeared, and her boyfriend is found mentally confused and unable to speak. She is never found, and the mystery is never resolved.

Thirty years later, Emily stands in the dark and hears an old man singing, calling out for "Darcie." She turns to see who is singing, but no one's there.

Join Emily as she is drawn deeper into discovering what happened to Darcie Malone.

Emily Menotti Mysteries are available on Amazon.com.